Red-wine moustache

written by Giorgia Cipolloni

Warnings: it contains substance abuse, suicidal tendencies, and way too many men.

Red-wine Moustache
ISBN: 9789403861845

This is dedicated to the Jazz Jam that plays relentlessly inside our heads.

Chapter I.

A candle's death (Blue Room)

A series of chaotic and yet truly heartfelt notes from Layla's diary:

There is something profoundly deadly, hidden in the tasks I execute every day. Getting through daily life is obnoxious. I shall be grateful. I feel ashamed of how hopeless I feel. I am bored. I am doing better than I thought I would, and yet, I am bored. Bored, bored, bored. And guilty of my privilege. I never felt at home, and I don't think I ever will. I am not entire: there are pieces of me in multiple places, and they will never collide. An irresolvable puzzle. I feel too much. I yearn too much. I want to know too much. I have been told I am, myself, too much. One day, I am gonna get myself a home, and everything will make sense. You know what I am talking about. You are a reflection of me — words of mine, son of mine. I am your mother. You are mine. However, I hope you don't misunderstand me. I don't exclusively despise routines per se; in fact, I recognize something deeply poetic in them. There is a very specific routine in my mind that I intend to live, eventually. One day, I will wake up, and I will rush out of bed to open the window that I have been waiting to open my entire life. One day, every kind of weather will come to me as a pleasant surprise. People usually look for a fresh start because they need to be a stranger. No expectations. For me, it's the opposite. I can't be true to myself here. People could only know me somewhere else, for I am not at home here. But one day, everything will change. One day, I will find that place. There is nothing else for me to do. That day, I will rush out of my bed, and whether I'll have the sun or the water, the blue, the grey, or the white, it will make sense. I'd wake up early, at around seven. I would then open the curtains. Breathe. Draw, make coffee, eat some fruit, and bake. At around eleven thirty, I would invite a friend over to complain about the government, and taste a new wine that I would carefully select from my small but powerful wine collection - by then, I would be an experienced oenophile. Afterwards, I would spend the rest of the day either making art or devouring it, and my hands would hold a new book every week. In the evening, at around nineteen, I would cook dinner for someone I love, hand them warm food as they say "fuck the fucking government", and close the curtains. I would then fall asleep under a warm blanket, held by a familiar pair of arms. I'd like to believe that such a routine would feel natural right away, but I fear that, as soon as I've been handed the keys to what I always wanted, I will dive into the depths of my loneliness. Perhaps, as soon as I've been handed the keys to go home, I will feel like my apartment is just a place to wait for something, for anything. Just like Anatole Broyard described in his memoir, Kafka Was The Rage. What would I do then? Even considering such a thing is dangerous for me. Imagine, for just a second, that I could spend my whole life waiting to achieve something, just to then be bored. Right now, it feels irrelevant, but soon, I will grow old.

It was a warm autumn day in Rome. That morning, Layla was mistaken for a professor by another student. She was carrying a brown *24-hour* bag that looked elegant and heavy, as she held two books in her hand that were unlikely to fit into the bag. She looked a bit older than her age, yet she had a childish trait within her presence: her dark hair, tied up with a red bow. As soon as she started high school, she began to understand how corrupt her world was.
The ceiling inside the classrooms of her school would break constantly, and, during her first semester there, a student got hit by a fallen panel and was hospitalised. The headmaster offered money to the student's family to keep them silent, and no one in Rome seemed to talk about it. Layla organised one protest after another, until eventually she founded a collective. Soon enough, even the professors were talking about her. Despite her contempt towards the Italian school system, her complete disinterest in grades, and her deep passion for artistic matters, when she started the collective, she was convinced to pursue a law career. *"This world is filled with injustice, and it is unjust because*

someone designed it this way on purpose. It is made by the rich, for the rich. The best way to help injustice lose power is then to either attempt to change the law, or to protect the unrepresented through more concrete actions," she used to say. Very shortly after that, she changed her mind and lost the last bit she had of institutional trust. Observing the world around her truly radicalized her.

A boy named Alex kept looking at her while she walked down the hallway. He admired and envied Layla for the amount of power she had been capable of gaining in so little time. Alex secretly wished he were her, or at least the idea he made in his mind of what Layla was like, based primarily on the research he did on her online and on the things he heard about her in school. He then went up to her.

"I'm rooting for you," Alex said.

Layla smiled. "Thank you!" she answered before walking away.

He thought she was bold. It was the third month of high school for both of them, and the first time they exchanged words. Alex and Layla both moved to town that September. What a timing! Oh timing…

Timing was everything. It was the reason why people would meet and die, it dictated expiration dates, and it provided death for candles. It is the reason why we trash food if we don't trust the number written on it, as well as the reason why fruit eventually turns brown, and humans eventually turn into dust.
Months, wars, but no words went by.
Layla had an obsession: noting down all the books that the people who crossed her path would read - on the subway, at the park, on a bench, sometimes even walking - then, after an accurate research, she would read them too. There were times when she would even read some of these books twice, although she didn't seem to know what she could achieve by doing that. Weren't the words she had previously read already supposed to be inside her?

On a winter day, Alex found Layla reading his favorite book: "*Noces - suivi de l'Eté*" by Albert Camus. She was sitting in the cafeteria of the school. "*I used to hate summer until I read these essays,*" Layla said, after Alex sat in front of her, in silence. He felt the same way about it, but he thought she wouldn't believe him if he told her.

Captured by their apparent similarity, Alex invited her to go and see a movie together. They watched *La Chinoise* by Jean-Luc Godard. They both adored Godard's nerve and Godard's dialogues. Sometimes, Alex and Layla would act like they were in one of those Nouvelle Vague films. They would dress as if they were in the sixties, and discuss the politics of that era, acting like it was their own. That kind of evening had a routine: the two would meet at Cavour Metro Station and walk to the cinema close to Piazza Barberini. Layla would complain that Alex walked too fast, then they would grab some dinner on the way back to Alex's place, where they would fall asleep, drunk and holding hands, fully dressed up.

In the morning, when the Sun was already high, Alex would take a double espresso with no milk or sugar, while Layla drowned her caffeine addiction in Oat Milk. They would then pick up a fight, Layla would shout something like *"Please! dance me to the end of Humanity,"* then leave Alex's dreamy apartment. They slowly, but not softly, became each other's closest soul. It was strange. Layla grew up in the countryside before moving into the city with her father. The first thing Alex noticed about Layla was that, sometimes, she looked extremely sad, or she would turn extremely sad, from one moment to the next, with no evident reason to provide to her surroundings. He found a guilty feeling of pleasure in thinking that Layla turned sad when observing strangers being happy while doing their grocery shopping with their family, for example. Layla was the daughter of a man, of a man only. Throughout her childhood, Layla longed for something to share with her father, but after a long search, all she found was exhaustion, or perhaps it was exhaustion that found her. It was like walking in what appeared to be an infinite desert, and morbidly trying to get attached to everything on her way: any plant, any animal, any rock, anything that wasn't just the sand, her very own name. Anything to share with her father that wasn't just her blood. She would cling to these things, to anything that she could discuss with Richard, and scream until her voice ran out, but Richard was never there to hear. Year after year, her research grew aggressive. Layla kept yearning to share that part of herself she only found in literature with her dad, while Richard used to say he *"didn't have time* to read," and he kept saying that he didn't have time for a lot of things until he ran out of it. Richard had a stroke while Layla was still in high school, and he died shortly after. He grew up in England in a boring English family, and he stayed there until he was thirty years old. He then went to Italy for a work trip, fell in love with the person who gave birth to Layla, and never returned to England again. It was Richard who named Layla after a song he liked. *"Layla"* was, in fact, an unusual name for an Italian lady. The only thing they had in common in this life, besides blood, was the good old music. Their music taste aligned through time. At first, Layla despised almost everything Richard would put on the radio, the same way he despised that outrageous yet indispensable rap music that Layla needed to hear when she was a young lady. Layla and Richard both dedicated their lives to a constant music in the background. When Richard died, Layla felt stuck and incapable of doing anything. That's when the jazz came along. Layla never felt like she truly needed her father; regardless of having no one else to rely on, she was always *"so good at being independent*", as Richard himself would say. Hence, she was confused by this state of immobility she was drowning in. She didn't stress too much about the funeral, partially because she was sick to her stomach, and partially because Richard wouldn't care either, as he always said people could do whatever with his ashes, as long as they wouldn't return them to England. A close friend of Richard's took care of the funeral. In return, Layla was asked to speak at the function. It was the end of the summer, and it was too hot in Rome to wear a suit. Everyone at the funeral was complaining about the weather, like every other hot summer day in Rome. When Layla walked up to the altar, close to where her father's grave lay open, she recalled a conversation they had had a couple of months before that.

"*When I die, you might as well let my funeral happen in a church. It's our culture. I don't care, as long as my ashes stay in this country,*" Richard said.
"*But you don't believe in god,*" she answered.
"*I doubt anyone truly believes in it; it's a fable.*"

Layla plucked up her courage and kissed her dead predecessor's forehead.

"To be loved is to be seen, and I don't think you ever saw me, father."

She then stood in silence, unaware of whether she pronounced her words out loud or not. Richard's friends were judging her. Needless to say, they never got along. One of them, an old, frustrated, lonely woman named Emma, even threatened to beat Layla to death when she was barely eleven and miserable. She was mad at Layla for wearing a crop top.
"You are ruining your father's life dressing like that, like a whore. I beat my children, and I wouldn't mind beating you, too. If I killed you, I wouldn't care. Your body is vulgar; you should cover it. You should know that. I don't care that we are at the swimming pool."

Layla took a deep breath and walked out of the church.
One week after Richard's death, Layla finally found the strength to clean their apartment. She then proceeded to trash stuff in the garbage and get some boxes ready, as she had to move somewhere cheaper. She believed that a move and a death were both a shift. The death of someone we love imposes a shift. There was a

Layla when Richard was alive, and there was a Layla when Richard was no longer.
She pictured her own existence like a cloth left out to dry that, once parched, belonged nowhere.
Moving again. How? Where? When would she have to move again? To shift again? Where to? Why? For how long? Alone?

That evening, Layla had the recurrent thought that she was sick inside and incapable of healing. Perhaps that thought itself was what made her sick. There were times in which, about her own life and about herself, all she could recall was her sickness. Whichever that was. Oh, how absurd it would be if, one day, all that would be remembered about Layla were her sickness. The thought of it made her nauseous.

She opened an old photo album and crumbled immediately. The first photo portrayed Richard on Christmas Day, one Christmas when Layla could've been four or five years old. He was wearing a chef's apron, holding what seemed like a giant turkey. Layla found herself in the right corner at the bottom of the picture. She is holding her dad's apron and looking at him with a simple and pure smile on her face. Her dad looked kind as tears began to travel down Layla's face. She proceeded to turn more pages of the photo album. In another picture, Richard was holding her just like he was holding the giant turkey in the previous photo. Layla used to fit in Richard's hand, like a little cat. Oh, the trust she had in her father then!

While shifting to a life without Richard, Layla had to resort to the use of distinctive and deadly coping mechanisms. One of them was jazz. She couldn't bring her ears anywhere close to any kind of rock music. For a whole month, Layla was never sober, but rather drunk with jazz and alcohol. She easily got access to a medical receipt that allowed her to get benzodiazepines. After spending an uncountable amount of time alone in a room that didn't feel like her room any longer, and staring at the ceiling that never felt so much her own, one day, one day, Layla ran out of her apartment and violently filled her own postbox with letters she had written while intoxicated, deprived of an address. It wasn't that the letters she wrote weren't meant to be sent somewhere, but rather that they belonged somewhere unknown. The place where Richard was, and the place a part of herself was condemned to be in, too.

That same evening, the housing agency that Layla was in contact with to sell the house called: the proceeds from the apartment could have covered the rent for a smaller apartment, for around three years. After a few weeks, Layla found a new, small studio somewhere in the south of Rome, and she moved in right away.

During her final years in high school, Layla worked as a waitress in three different restaurants - all of which she despised. It wasn't necessarily the job that she didn't like. It was just too easy to get a rude, old, and gross Italian boss. To Layla, being a waitress was like being an actress. At first, she enjoyed playing the part, since she could decide her role. She used to pick a different name and a different story every time a customer was acting way too curious. *"Are you from here?" "What's your name?" "You speak so many languages! Your parents must be so proud,"* and so on. Layla soon mastered her: *"Yes, I am from Rome. Oui, I do speak French, too. Yes, I visited*

Paris." and *"Yes, just like the song." "Yes, I am young. Yes, I am a student. YES, they are VERY proud."* At times, she would force a French accent and say, *"I just moved here. No, I don't like the city. Bah ouais, in France everything is better."* Other times she would go for a *"Si, I moved here from Spain. My husband cheated on me, and we have a three-year-old son. I look younger than I am, I'm aware."* Eventually, she became tired even of her own stories, and the tips weren't great either. Thereupon, Layla knew that, in order to survive in that city, she would need to run away every once in a while.

Alex's mother was a film director. He grew up loved by a father who wasn't biological. It was evident. You could see it by the way he tried to bond with others. He would ask a lot of questions and provide small gifts to the people who played the characters in his life. It was obvious that he was trying to be loved, and that he was, and a lot. Alex cared more about being loved by the people he wanted to bond with, rather than getting to know them for what they were, and he was, somewhere very deep inside of him, aware of that, and not ashamed of it. He was the kind who cared more about his acknowledgment of things when asking questions, rather than getting something out of them.

For Alex, there were two kinds of questions: those you ask because you want to acknowledge something, and those you ask because you want the answerer to acknowledge something. Alex wouldn't usually try to move the people and the things around him as much as the things inside of him. He was convinced that "*we all live alone inside ourselves, in the end.*" He would, however, get mad if someone else tried to get something out of him. Alex always preferred *receiving words* rather than *providing words* to someone else. That is why he became Layla's friend. The two spent most of their time together reading, drinking wine, or going to the cinema. Layla was never silent around him, and Alex somehow got the impression that Layla wanted him to get closer to her.

Layla used to write a lot of letters. During their fourth year of high school, she wrote nine letters to Alex only. He only got one of the letters she wrote, the first one:

"To whom call me Layla and not Lay,

for

he knows my real name.

The first time I saw you sleep,
I already found you unbearable.

Perhaps we were together because we were lonely;
perhaps we weren't together at all
- though you did kiss my forehead, stronzo

The second time I saw you sleep,
We were as fragile as crystal glasses…

I remember feeling your hand,
and the sunlight on your finger
in the morning.

I remember your dark hair falling on the pillows
then seeing the clouds through your windows
I never felt intimacy before."

Alex read that one on an annoying evening, as it was lying in between the pages of Layla's green notebook. They were drinking red wine in

Via Nazionale, and he grabbed it. Layla was unsure whether he realized that the letter was written for him. Maybe he knew. He doubtless knew a lot of things. He knew how to make her go crazy, and he knew how to brush his teeth. He knew what film to watch, when to watch it, and how to review them. More important than the things he knew were the things he didn't know. He didn't know how to make Layla feel safe; perhaps he didn't mean to. He didn't know when to stop with his bloody questions. He didn't know how to bake a cake or how to properly use an oven. Layla didn't know many things either: she had no idea about what to do when sick. She didn't know if her way of washing cutlery and dresses was the proper way. She didn't know if Alex, or anyone, could be trusted. If Alex couldn't truly read her, who would? How can someone learn how to translate their pain?

After quickly reading the letter, Alex made a joke about Layla's red-wine moustache.

"Is everyone destined to be understood by at least one person, or is my sick mind truly alone?", Layla wrote down in her green notebook, before putting it

back into her purse, right after Alex read that page. That night, she went back to her small, uneventful studio apartment only to deal with her pain. As soon as she entered her studio, she sat on the floor, and she cried, unable to breathe, and fully aware she was having a panic attack. She then had a series of rolling panic attacks. After an hour and a half, she was scared and considered calling the ambulance, but she didn't want to call it for something that wasn't urgent. Somewhere else in Rome, someone else needed it more. She then attempted to call Alex once or twice, but he did not answer. She kept drinking water while trying to calm down, but it didn't work as it usually would. After two of the longest hours of her life, Layla got in the shower and sat still under the warm water for a while, and fell asleep there. She woke up with the water still flowing underneath her feet, as well as the feeling of guilt for the water wasted. Finally, she got out of the shower, put on a shirt, and went to bed. She knew she was alone. All of the stuff she put in her studio wouldn't help make it a home. Most of the people entering her studio would tell Layla, *"This is very you!"*, and she would have to force a smile and hide the painful truth that came with it. She couldn't do anything to make that place more welcoming. She kept looking at her things while trying to rest: the red bra on her lamp, the candles on the desk, the photographs that were all over the walls, the pavement, and even between her books… Was it her? What was it that made a place her own? And if she could be a place, what would it look like? Would she like it? Would she feel at home?

All the candles and the cozy lighting in the world would not make a home, Layla knew that. She carefully observed the candle on her bedside table consume itself until it blew out, and she finally fell asleep, breathing the intoxicating scent of that candle's demise.

Chapter II.

Alex (My Funny Valentine)

He had severe anxiety and a noisy stomach. Both of them were diagnosed by the best doctors in town. His classmates used to call him *'Kafka'* and think of him as a loser. Alex did not care, for he knew who he was. It was Alex's typical summer evening, as he was in San Lorenzo Square, drinking an Italian beer with the pleasurable company of three books and the Italian chaos in the background. Funny enough, two of these books were written by Kafka. A man in his seventies headed closer to Alex, curious about what he was reading.
After standing in front of him for a gentle amount of time, the man asked Alex what sounded like a billion different questions that Alex didn't quite understand. Alex, who secretly enjoyed writing, felt the need to provide a story for him. The old man seemed kind, but he couldn't understand a word of what Alex was telling him.

"Giovanotto, cosa leggi?"
"Kafka,"
"Non ti capisco. Sei qui tutto solo, perché?"

"Sto leggendo Kafka, signore."
"Che peccato, non ti capisco. Io alla tua età il sabato sera lo passavo a fare altro. O è forse un martedì?" asked the old man, before leaving.

That brief encounter bothered Alex, and it left a sense of misunderstanding in the air that he did not have the capacity to bear. Alex had no idea what the old man was trying to tell him. Did he mean that a young man should be busy writing stories rather than reading someone else's? Was he not aware that people's stories are all we've got? What is left of a story that no one wants to hear?

Walking towards that dark and rich apartment in which he was living, Alex kept thinking, *"Reading and writing go hand in hand, although they do not intend the same thing." "Reading and writing go hand in hand, although they do not intend the same thing," "Reading and writing go hand in hand, although they do not intend the same thing."*
"Paradoxically, perhaps it is easier to be appreciated as a writer than as a reader", Alex thought, while entirely lost in his mind. He never talked about it, and he acted like he didn't notice it, but he had a particular condition for which when he

felt misunderstood by the person he was talking to, or he felt unwanted in some way, his words would come out of his mouth for himself rather than for the interlocutor (yes, just like his bloody questions), and the people would somehow find it difficult to understand what he would say. As a consequence, Alex would slowly lower his voice, making it even more difficult to understand him.

The path to his apartment was dark enough for Alex to feel comfortable in it. He was lucky to be a male. He suddenly felt the need to scream so intensely that he considered getting in a car and heading to the nearest beach. The beach of Ostia was only thirty minutes away, but he couldn't provide himself with the energy his mind was yearning for. He kept walking in the dark, unable to put his mind to rest, despite the weather of Rome matching his own. He even ran for about a mile without knowing why, and without anticipating it. It wasn't uncommon for Alex to deal with emotions he was unable to describe. If he couldn't put his feelings into words, then he didn't know what to do with them. For that reason, he needed constant distractions. Alex tried every sport he could think of and at least a different hobby every week. During the past month, Alex went sailing, tried ceramics classes, and seriously considered beginning to study Russian. He enjoyed doing ceramics, but he wasn't good enough, and the weather would soon get bad for a beginner sailor to properly learn how to sail on the big, wide sea, or so he told himself, as an excuse for not pursuing it. As for Russian, he had no excuse: he just didn't want it enough. He was already enrolled in a French course, anyway. Soon, he would be able to read *"Noces"* in French, just like Layla. No one could try to separate Alex from Camus. Not even his increasing political awareness.

He finally arrived at his flat, and, right at the corner of the door, the tiredness assaulted him. He could barely open the door before collapsing into his bed.

When he woke up, he looked around. On the side of his bed, there was a huge window facing a yellow and pink-colored Roman street. The sunlight was heavy on his naked chest and kindly caressed his eyes. He was in the mood for a bowl of fruit and felt strangely curious to taste flowers for breakfast, too. He put on a record by Eric Dolphy and danced around while getting ready. His bathroom had blue-colored walls and white bricks around the mirror. There was a window in the shower's ceiling, so the sun could highlight the shampoo on Alex's hair. He dried up, then gently buttoned up his light blue blouse and ran downstairs to get fruit at the local market.

The blessing of light will soon provide him with fresh stories.

Layla called Alex then. It was around nine in the morning, and her voice cracked. She couldn't explain what was going on, because *"nothing was going on"*. Alex took a taxi and got stuck in the traffic. It took him a whole hour to get to her studio.

Alex rang the doorbell before noticing that Layla's door was open. She was sitting on the floor, in front of her bed, staring at nothing. Alex closed the door.

"I am sorry, there was a lot of traffic," he said.

"Thank you for being here. I am sorry, I can already taste how pathetic I will be today. Could you pass me the water? I ran out."

Alex filled a glass of water that Layla didn't drink. He then looked around and with his eyes meant: *"What are you waiting for?"*

"If I drink it, I will choke," she explained to him.

Alex then sat on the floor next to his friend.

"Are you going to tell me what is going on? Anything I should know about? Is it Richard? Is it work? Perhaps a new lover? Or even school? Did you fail an exam or something? We're close to graduation…"

"As if I ever cared about that."

"Some of us care."

"Well, you don't have much else to worry about, do you?"

"Wow. Thank you. I wonder what my parents - whom you seem to like very much - would think of that."

"Did you come here to argue with me?"

"Layla, you are insane. I swear, sometimes I'd like to choke you with my own hands."

Layla's eyes were absent until that moment, when they finally filled with tears.

"Does anyone else know you? Do I know you, Alex?"

He didn't respond. He didn't understand.

A few minutes of silence followed.

"You don't owe me anything. I regret calling you," Layla said.
"You are welcome, despite everything, *I do care,"* Alex replied.

Alex ordered some food from a restaurant.
"Let's eat something," said Alex, as he handed Layla two spring rolls.
"The table is a mess," Layla pointed out.
"Who cares? We'll eat on the floor."
"I wonder what your mother would think of that."
"Thanks, Lord, for at least one of us can ask themselves that."

The two laughed. Alex was good, sometimes. Despite their frequent misunderstandings, there was something ironic worth preserving there, between them. A sort of complicity. How lucky they were to have a "who cares? We'll eat on the floor" kind of friendship.
They ate everything Alex bought in under ten minutes.

"So... what the fuck happened?"
"I need a distraction; I don't need to think about it."
"You are not aware of what you need, sometimes it is good to tal-,"
"Alex, no, please," interrupted Layla.

"It is Richard, isn't it?"
"It's not it."
"Are you facing financial problems? Do you need money?"
"I do not, and you know that I would never ask. I would find another way that doesn't involve you."
"I bet you would. I got you a new book. Well, an old book. A new old book."

Alex took *Briefe An Milena* from his tote bag.

A natural, genuine smile appeared on Layla's face.

"Guess you might be Kafka after all," she said.

She looked at the beautiful old German edition that Alex got her, then she rolled her eyes. It was her way of saying *"thank you"*.

"I knew you would've wanted to read it in German, you Xenophile."
"Is it possible that you just did something right?"

Layla looked at him. He was wearing her favorite of all of his blouses, the blue one that he got for his birthday. He was quite beautiful, carrying within himself as much beauty as annoyance.

"If I disappeared, would you look for me?"
"What do you have in mind?"
"I am wondering. If one day you woke up and I was nowhere to be found, would you look for me?"

"Perhaps," Alex took a deep breath. "*...after a while,*" he added.

Alex knew what she wanted to hear, but he didn't know what she meant.
"By the way, there is a Godard review at the cinema in my neighborhood, and I think we should go," Alex said.
"When does it begin?"
"Tonight."
"Okay. Do you want to spend your day with me?"
"I could, but I would need to cancel French class."
"Right, I forgot about that. You should leave soon, then. I will meet you later at the cinema."
Alex got up and left, loudly. Layla sat on her bed with her legs up the wall and her face slightly outside the mattress. Her hair was almost touching the ground. She got to her sink and cut her hair until it was a long bob.
It was time to get clean. Godard was waiting.
That night, Roma was filled with rainwater. When it rains that much, you can see the reflection of the lights on the ground of the city, a thing that both Layla and Alex always adored.
Once the movie was over, Layla and Alex walked out, arm in arm. Layla's new haircut made her hair appear straighter than usual.
"I decided we are going to be Jean-Luc Godard and Anna Karina," announced Layla.
"Oh, Dio Mio, stop."

"We look like them... kind of... just look at my hair!"

Alex looked at Layla. He knew something wasn't right at all.

"Fine, Anna."

Layla did her best to avoid looking at him, but she smiled.

They walked in silence for a while, then Layla asked:

"Where do you think life is happening? For I don't believe that's here."

Alex seemed slightly annoyed by Layla's sudden change of humor. He thought they were having a good time. That's when Layla began one of her exhausting monologues.

"I am sorry if you find this pathetic, but please just try to get close to what I mean and try to answer. Where is life happening? Sometimes, I feel like I have everything - I am aware of my privilege, yet I can't help but be bored. Some other times, I don't have the time to be bored, but I still feel like I am slightly annoyed by something I can't fully acknowledge. Where is life happening? In some small beach? Or in someone's home? I don't mean a physical place necessarily, as long as it's a home. Close to a beach. Or perhaps in the mountains. Should I move to the mountains? You could bring me books when you visit," Layla said, as she

fantasized about a life she would never get to live. For just a second, she considered asking out loud whether she was alone. Somewhere deep down inside of her, she knew Alex couldn't answer that. Only she could.

"Life is happening wherever you are busy thinking about all these things," concluded Alex.

Chapter III.
Absurd Theory (Days of Wine and Roses)

The sky was white: winter had arrived, and Layla seemed paralyzed. She had just fought with Alex, and she was overwhelmed by the huge amount of things she felt she had to do. However, she had no intention of doing any of these things that day, as she had dropped everything, looking for some dopamine.
Even though she could feel the breeze through her hair, she looked completely absent. An American man in his mid-twenties named Daniel was driving Layla around Rome on a red Vespa.
Layla met Daniel by fate. She was wandering around Trastevere when she noticed a man on the corner of the street. He looked like he was about twenty-three or so; he had quite long brown curly hair, and he always wore glasses. When Layla first met him, she felt something she acknowledged as dangerous right away, and she was sure she was going to see him again.

The first night they were ever in the same place, the mysterious man and Layla didn't exchange a single word. Layla kept thinking about him during the upcoming days; it was a guilty pleasure of hers, having a silly interest in a stranger. After all, that was a pretty solid distraction from capitalism. She always had to work, think, argue, produce, paint, listen, or learn. Sometimes, life felt like a burden. There is no harm in looking for a reason to do all of that, and there are times in which a reason can be someone else.

Forty-seven days later, Layla met him again, this time, in a jazz bar. Daniel had just gotten back from New York. He played the saxophone in a band, or two, or three. Their eyes met multiple times during the concert. The first time, it was up to Layla, as she was shamelessly staring at him playing. She wanted to get involved in the art of playing the saxophone and understand it enough for her to believe she could fully swim inside of it. How pretentious. The second time their eyes met, Daniel initiated a smile at her, or so Layla thought. The third time, their eyes appeared to be longing for each other. She decided to leave, though she kept looking at him while stepping backwards to get the coat hanger and then, out of the door.

The madness began when Layla flew to Poland in the following October. She was visiting an old friend, and Daniel happened to be playing a concert downtown. A sweet and sharp coincidence. Layla's friend had left her that afternoon, so she had the rest of the day to explore Krakow. She had a coffee in the Main Square, then walked all over the Old Town until she found a small bar with live music.

The walls of that Polish jazz bar had bricks all over them. The color grey reigned inside there. Daniel was there. He noticed her right away, but he didn't have the guts to pronounce a single letter out loud. While she was appreciating the jazz, Layla couldn't help but stare at the bricks. The owner of the bar was a maximalist Polish Lady named Maja. Maja worked there as a bartender, too, and she always had a cigarette in her hand. She gathered a lot of furniture in there, and she filled the place with small paintings and tied vintage women's shoes to the ceiling. There was even a mirror ball, as well as candles everywhere. Red and Pink roses were present on every table, and they looked particularly romantic, surrounded by all that

smoke. Layla just had enough wine for her to decide that living was worth it all. Life was beautiful, truly. As beautiful as artists are. Maja offered Layla a cigarette.
She lit it and looked at Daniel. Layla wanted to sincerely understand how his hands, his fingers, and his nerves functioned. She wanted to grasp the way they were designed and how perfectly they had to be organised, for them to produce art through touch. She yearned to be inside his art and inside his mind. It was then that Layla gave jazz permission to inspire her to produce art. She would dive so deep into the music that it could provide her with visions for future photoshoots. It wasn't even necessary for her to close her eyes; she could easily picture what she wanted to shoot next, from her ears.

Lately, Layla had decided to bring a pen and a sketchbook with her, everywhere she went. On that wooden table and chair in the corner, she was drawing so intensively that she spilled enough ink on her hands for them to resemble the most chaotic constellations. Some people at the bar came and talked to her, curious about

what she was drawing, boldly assuming she was doing it for attention.
It was quite the opposite: she felt like she was the only guest inside there. There was an immense need for solitude amidst that crowd. Daniel decided to engage in conversation with Layla, quite out of the blue*s*.

"I see you in jazz bars all around Europe with your diary, it almost seems like you constantly need to be somewhere else," said Daniel to Layla for the very first time.
"Not when you are playing," she answered, while breathing in Maja's cigarette.
Daniel was taken by surprise. "What's your name?" he asked.
"I am Layla. And you are Daniel. I know." As soon as Layla pronounced these words, the concert break ended, and Daniel had to go back to his saxophone.
The mirror ball was restless, while Layla was calm, mesmerized, inside her young, dreamy mind. Her head truly was in the clouds when Daniel was playing. "*I riflettori facevano l'amore con la sua pelle*", she noted down.

Layla took a xanax from her bag and kept messing around with the pen, *"He who produces art on stage is Death's opponent, as Death begins when the lights are off"*. The pavement was trembling along with the beat of the hearts present in the room. She felt alive again.

Il freddo si sente a dicembre, si soffre a marzo./ The coldness is felt in December, but suffered in March
All night long
dancing between street lamps
fear, she only felt
of tomorrow.
Layla feared only
The future, Layla,
che si trasportava, addosso, la Layla del rimorso/ who transported, within' herself, the Layla of Regrets

Fear, she only felt
of her morning self
that Layla of tomorrow,
the one with no ringtone
between the dressing-up chaos
thinking about the masks
She wore the previous day
One feels the cold in December, but suffers it in March. On a sunny day.

Layla learned in school that Kierkegaard thought that life could be understood only by looking at the past, and lived only by looking forward to the future. When Layla was sick, she believed in the opposite. She was convinced that life could also be understood by looking at the future, and lived in our past, as the present turns into the past faster than we'd accept it, and some humans are condemned to relive their past each day. She thought it was true that someone's past could tell a lot about their present, but she believed in the other way around, too. Someone's present could also help people better understand their past. A lot of people who grew up surrounded by violence grew up to be extremely kind.

Despite *the Damned Time* having the power to alter human memories, or perhaps because of it, Layla would usually recall her past brighter than it was. The future was blank for everyone. A human's perspective had the power to change everything. When Layla thought about her own position and perspective, she thought she was one of these people who *"suffered the cold in March"*. Layla always thought that the cold was supposed to be felt in December, but suffered in

March. One expects December to be cold where she is from. On the other hand, March is expected to be warm. That is why Layla always suffered from the cold in March.

After the concert, Daniel went back to Layla.
"I think it is fun that I heard you playing in Rome, and we first exchanged words here in Krakow," she told him.
The place was getting empty. There were candles slowly burning their edges, petals of dead roses falling on the tables, and lights being turned up. The lipstick stain Layla left on her wine glass was now more visible than before, and she had a *red-wine moustache.*

"I think it's absurd. Do you live in Rome?" he asked.
"Yes."
"Why are you here? I mean…" - a brief silence followed *"between all the places that could be in, this is quite a coincidence,"* stated Daniel.
"I am visiting an old friend. Some lady I met somewhere ages ago."
"Ages ago? You look so young."
"Well, I believe time does not pass equally for everyone," she fiercely answered.

"You have a point here. How long are you staying in Poland?"

"I am leaving tomorrow. As it turns out, I don't get along well with that old friend of mine as I did back in the day."

"Let's go then," said Daniel. He enjoyed acting way more confident than he was. In fact, he found Layla was quite intimidating at first.

Layla thought about it for a moment before standing up. Daniel followed her outside.

They weren't expressing much out loud through words. Daniel briefly introduced himself: he was American, more precisely, he was a New Yorker, even more precisely, he was *a guy* from Bushwick. He could play the saxophone, the piano, and the guitar. He moved to Rome to be closer to the European Jazz scene, and he was unsure about where he was going with his life, as if someone had a clue. Layla also said something about herself: she lived all of her life in Rome, she was working two jobs while studying, she left the city every time she had a chance, and she was yearning to change her life entirely. She was still stuck in Rome because she didn't know how to snap out of it.

They walked all over Krakow Old Town, then they stopped on a bridge, where Daniel kissed her gently.
"My hotel is right around the corner. Would you want to spend the night?" he said.
Krakow in October can get quite chilly at night. She decided she trusted him.
Once in the room, as they were on the sofa, Daniel touched Layla's hand and gave her a forehead kiss, she pretended not to notice. They fell asleep while watching a movie, the same way two old friends who feel like home would do.
At 5 a.m., Layla woke up. Daniel was sleeping. The sunlight highlighted the kisses Layla's lipstick left on Daniel's skin in the dark. She then tore out a page of her favorite notebook and wrote down something for Daniel to read once he'd wake up. She took a last look at Daniel and closed the door behind her. She had an airplane to catch.

Seventy days passed.
Layla found herself hearing Daniel playing live again, this time, in Rome. Daniel was capable of making his own breathing feel like comfort.

Layla was fantasizing about slitting her wrists open.
She was terrified. She wasn't the kind of artist capable of changing muse: if something went wrong with Daniel, along with her idea of him, her art should have died too. As she stared at the bar's candles, she thought that, by having a muse, she was condemning her art in the same way that a candle that, once lit, is condemned to die. Daniel became a part of her from the first day she saw him. The thought of ever losing *whatever that was* made her sick to her stomach. She had no idea what she could do once her art, her candle, was close to the end.
Being involved with Daniel, she thought, was like a pleasant wait that would, at times, make her feel like out of place; Other times, she felt so involved that all she could do was wait for the end. She feared the day concerts would resemble funerals, and an instrument would appear as a ghost. She feared the day the red wine at the jazz club, already old and vaguely disgusting, would have become too warm to drink. Would the music still communicate to her then?

The sky wouldn't turn grey that day, though its color wouldn't matter to Layla anymore. The music coming from anybody else's movement wouldn't matter. The words Layla and Daniel exchanged wouldn't matter. Only ghosts would matter then.

Layla noticed her own veins moving to Daniel's rhythm. They were both filled with wine and blood. Her black lace dress covered her legs up to her knees, and it had no sleeves. Everything around and inside of her was flowing. She felt as beautiful as fragile.

After the concert, Daniel pretended to have missed his bus to talk with Layla. He went to the jazz bar on his scooter, and Layla was aware that his scooter was parked. The weather was white and anonymous, such a sky was unusual for Roma, and such a meeting too. It was a big city, after all. Daniel was wearing a grey suit and a brown jacket that didn't quite fit the rest of his outfit.

Layla learned to know him: he adored Bill Evans and furniture made of wood. He smoked tobacco when he felt under pressure, and he never smoked before a concert. In a certain way, he felt at ease only in jazz, free from any form of chains. He knew a lot of people, but he often felt alone. Too diverse, too much of this, too little of that. From the outside, you couldn't tell he was an outsider at heart. He was often laughing with the people at the bar. If someone he knew came with the company of someone he didn't know, Daniel would make sure to introduce himself. In this regard, he was quite different from Layla. She was often quiet, despite being bold and extroverted.

A few days passed.
While sitting in the back of Daniel's Vespa, Layla tried to visualize her future, but she saw nothing: she could not imagine herself in 20 years, not even in 10. The thought of working for her whole life was such an absurd realization in her mind. She did not have a particular interest that was worth fulfilling all her days, throughout her life. She envied Daniel for having something he was good at and loved to dedicate himself to entirely. The society Layla was a part of was meaningless to her. Authenticity was fading away. And so was she, or at least, so she thought.

"*I can't breathe!*" Layla said in a trembling voice. Daniel insinuated she was about to have a panic attack, so he had to pull up next to a supermarket and buy her some water.
"*Do you feel any better now?*"
"*Si. Let's go to the jazz club.*"

Layla adored the sense of liberty and freedom that jazz music was capable of giving her. More than that, the comfort it would provide. Her favorite jazz bar in Rome didn't even have a proper name. It was simply called "*il jazz bar*". The walls were red, and there were candles on every table, except for the table in the left corner, which was dedicated to musicians and always covered by instruments during the breaks. There were cozy green lamps on the floor and at the entrance door.
Sometimes Daniel would take Layla on his scooter around Rome with no specific destination, even though they would almost always end up in Layla's favorite jazz club, whether he was going to play or not. Layla slept at Daniel's that night. One particular thing about Daniel is that he would always end his

day by falling asleep to drum sets. He would play exclusively drum beats for the whole night. The first night they slept together, back in Poland, Layla thought it might have been a way to get rid of her, but it wasn't. He was holding her tight. It was unexpected for someone who plays everything but the drums to fall asleep to a drum beat. Some people might think of drums as an instrument they want to hear when trying to wake up, rather than when trying to fall asleep, but not Daniel. He was the opposite.

The morning afterwards, Layla didn't want to stay with Daniel nor go back to where her belongings were, therefore she took a train and went to the sea. The sun coloring Ostia Beach looked like a fading memory. It was pure chaos: clouds and stars coexisting. There were old, ugly white buildings surrounding the seashore, and closed bars that would soon open again. It was March, which means that the water wasn't too cold, but the people would still rather stay home. She sat on the sand, fascinated by the water. She enjoyed the sound of the waves until her mind came up with the picture of the waves turning the color of blood. She didn't mind that kind of red; She dreamed of riding the red waves until the very last tear of her own blood. She would feel the pulse in her heart and the pressure of the ocean, and she would finally be in control of it. Swimming into her own blood, she would then feel safe. When her thoughts became too intense, Layla decided to leave. She walked towards that station with her headphones at the highest level of volume, causing herself a panic attack. Once in the station, she went to the public toilet just to find out that it was locked. *Fucking Roma.* There was no escape: everybody could see her. Yes, everybody could see her as everybody who looked at her knew she was not doing fine. There wasn't anything hurting her in particular, except for her existence. Unsolicited pain. These kinds of panic attacks were the worst. Suddenly, she was thinking about all the friends she lost, all the places she will never explore, and all the lovely people she will never meet. Not to mention all the words and all the art she will never be able to consume. It comes with no warning or expectations, Life and all the lives we will never get to live. How unbereable, how magnific.

Despite Layla's usual success of being a credible absurdist, it was easy for her to fall back into Existentialism, or worse, into Nihilism. To everyone who ever cared enough to get to know her, she would explain her *"absurd theory"* by stating, *"One starts with Nihilism. It is clear, we look for answers that do not matter. Next stop, Existentialism. Why do we even care that those answers don't matter? Finally, Absurdism and the embracement of this absurd existence we are all condemned to live."*

The train was late, as usual. Layla checked her wallet: she had five euros cash, a picture dated five years earlier, back to when she had red hair, a couple of notes, and a credit card with less than twenty euros on it - there was no way of getting a taxi. She looked up at the train departures board; it was now forty-five minutes delayed. Layla's shoes were full of sand, and her hands felt dry and salty.

As she headed to the ticket desk, she recalled a butterfly she saw that morning and wondered where butterflies go when it's windy. How rare it is to see a butterfly, yet they're always somewhere. Perhaps that's what Layla should have done. Focus on the fact that there were butterflies flying somewhere, despite the wind, despite their hiding.

She then reached the vending machine and got some water, assuming it would help her calm down. Then she called Alex twice. That bastard only replied on the third attempt.

"Alex! Where do you think butterflies go when it's windy?" she asked.

"What?" replied Alex with no specific intonation, confused but not surprised.

"Where do they go?" she insisted, in a way that made her sound like she was excited to find out, almost as if she were a little girl.

Alex thought about it. That sounded serious.

"Somewhere safe," he stated.

"Grazie."

She then hung up the phone and looked for her track. Layla had a book with her, as she would usually do, but she finished it twenty minutes before the train would arrive, so she opened her sketchbook and started drawing the people around her. Layla kept drawing all the way back to her apartment, even while walking, only to find out she had been drawing herself, masked as every stranger she thought she drew.

Chapter IV.
Lawrence, on and off stage (Strange Fruit)

Layla and Daniel sat one in front of the other, and it seemed that they were floating in the air, occupying zero physical space. Stars danced around as Layla was entirely lost in Daniel. Daniel saw her as Beatrice used to see Dante – "*… ella, che vedea me sì com'io…*", capable of reading him just as he could himself (La Divina Commedia, Primo Canto del Paradiso). Layla closed the jazz bar that night. And then, every night of the week. After three weeks, she had met all of the usual musicians of the club. One particularly sick night, when Layla was drunk and sad, an older piano player, probably in his sixties, went to talk to her between sets. Layla recognized him soon enough; He was a regular musician there and one of the best pianists she ever heard, *so good he almost was music himself,* some poet might argue.

His name was Lawrence, and he grew up in Harlem, in New York City. Lawrence approached her as a caring grandpa would do. His warmth was imminent, and everyone around him knew that. He intended to introduce Daniel to Layla, unaware of the fact that they had already met. Lawrence always had something to tell about his past and rarely something to tell about his present. From that night on, every evening, after playing his adored piano, he would get wine with Layla and the other musicians (this often included Daniel) in the "backstage" (the jazz bar in question is so small that addressing that as a backstage feels illegal), narrate one or two stories about his past in the Big Apple, then he would stand up and say *"An early morning is waiting for me, see you next time"* and leave. No one knew what Lawrence was busy doing in the daylight. Daniel once almost dared to ask, only to be interrupted by Lawrence patting his shoulder. No one ever dared ask him again.

Notes flew all around, again. Layla noticed that whenever Lawrence was about to play, he would leave his eyeglasses on the piano. She secretly always wanted to photograph it. It was very interesting: every time, his glasses would assume a different position and invoke a different movement. It felt like Lawrence's glasses could make the world capable of seeing him better, even from afar, instead of making him see the world better. Later, when Layla confronted other people about it, she found out no one else had noticed Lawrence's glasses lying on the piano. It shocked her. To her, that was a very distinctive trait of Lawrence's being. Lawrence was on stage, so his eyeglasses were on stage. Lawrence was playing, so his eyeglasses were dancing - or rather, resisting, to it. Sometimes, Layla would notice the glasses' presence in the jazz bar even before noticing Lawrence.

Daniel, Lawrence, and Layla were all sitting at the bar. Lawrence openly recalled a time, while he was living in Harlem, and he was just a eleven-years-old homeless kid sleeping in the streets, on some stairs. It must have been sometime between November and February, as it was snowing, and he was freezing. He was not alone; two of his friends were with him: Trevor and Leo. Trevor was the youngest of the group; he was barely nine, and he was the only child of a single mom. Leo was the oldest; he was sixteen, or seventeen, perhaps. No one was ever sure about anything regarding Leo. He escaped from some place at some point and never looked back. Lawrence said Leo lived in Texas for ten years and then moved to NYC on his own after a long hitchhike ride. That night, a lady in a fancy red dress met them and gave them blankets. Her name was Angela, and she acted accordingly. She told them she knew what it was like for those kids, as she grew up in a similar situation, too. It was Christmas time, and she thought it wasn't fair that some children were not going to receive any gifts; therefore, she asked them what they desired. Leo, who was not only the oldest but also the wisest, asked for a job. Trevor asked for a kite. Lawrence asked for a piano. Angela came back after a couple of hours with a kite. She then took them to her small flat in the Bronx and told them that they could live there, as long as they "behaved" and kept the flat clean. The kids were skeptical, but they agreed. The flat had a piano inside, just in front of the window. It was quite used, but the sound was great. The kids were less scared than they were before, and unaware that they would soon address each other as family.

Being abundantly moved by that story, Layla's face got wet with tears in the middle of the jazz club. She had long practiced how to cry in silence, and only Lawrence noticed she cried. He then went back on stage, leaving Layla alone with her thoughts and all the questions she didn't dare to ask him. She would easily lose her mind. A minor change of anything had the potential to provoke her destructive thoughts. Even less. A small, insignificant detail could be enough to bring her life to a dangerous perspective on a bad night. It was hard to get certain thoughts to go away. In the same way, a positive minor detail could also change everything and dictate her mood for a long time. Nobody knew what was going on inside her mind, perhaps not even her. Layla always thought of herself as someone easy to read and quite transparent, especially with Daniel, but she was actually slightly confusing and often misunderstood. For example, certain nights, she wouldn't even dare say "*Hello*" to Daniel; Other nights, she would feel like dying if she didn't end the day by gently drowning in his arms. She was sincere enough to be incapable of faking a smile. Easy things could easily make her happy: a rose, a letter, an unexpected gesture. Easy things could easily make her sad, too. It wasn't the surprises that made her unhappy, but rather the ordinary things - the love that surrounded the streets, the children who played in the park, and all the things she owned. These things are what made her feel like she was dying. She knew that she didn't need to end her life, but rather start a new one, or perhaps change perspective, or whatever it was that was wrong with her mind. She could run to New York and provide a sense of familiarity to Lawrence's stories. Bring them to life. She could walk Lawrence's steps in his honor, and then disappear. She would have approached whoever crossed her mind, whenever they crossed her mind. She would constantly throw out all of her words, without thinking too deeply about it, and she wouldn't need to dream anymore. *New York, how pathetic!* Layla felt homologated, and she was irremediably distant from herself. She could surely find a solution that did not involve New York if she only needed to disappear. There must have been a cloud dense enough to cover her whole being, somewhere. It got to the point that Layla had to tell herself, *"Layla, there is nothing else you could be. You can't go past this. This is all you are and all you could ever be. Put an end to it."* She wanted to erase herself, get rid of all of her clothes, all of her records, even her most beloved literary taste, and start again, from zero.

The concert ended, Layla and the band got drinks, before she and Daniel headed towards Daniel's place. *"Did you know about Trevor and Leo?"* Layla asked.

"I have known Lawrence for years, and yet, the more he tells me, the less I feel like I know him. He mentioned many people from the Bronx, but he never mentioned them."

A moment of silence followed as the two kept walking. Layla's steps were loud.

"I actually believe he is more open with us when you are present… I think he wants you to know him," said Daniel.

A little girl went next to Daniel, walking faster and faster while looking at him, perhaps challenging him to run. He was intrigued and picked up the pace. When they finally arrived, Daniel opened the door and invited Layla inside through a polite hand gesture and a small, friendly bow. In a comforting silence, the two brushed their teeth together and got ready to go to bed. Daniel reached for Layla's hand. After some hours, when she reached for Daniel's hand, as he was sleeping, he turned his back the other way. It was a gesture that probably meant nothing, and yet it was enough for her to unfriend the soft, shared silence they built. She did not sleep much that night. How could people find joy in holding a hand that could turn their back at any moment?

A couple of weeks passed. Layla was strolling between bookstores when she met Lawrence, on his way to rehearsal.

"Lawrence! Hi!"

At first, Lawrence didn't seem to recognize her. It wasn't a unique thing; it happened quite often, with everyone. Sometimes, he didn't look like he was awake. They talked about it once, Lawrence, Layla, and Daniel. The pianist explained that there were days in which waking up was the hardest task he could bear for the day, and that his brain was aware of it, and that that was the reason why sometimes he wouldn't recognize people. He was never trying to be rude; he was merely trying to survive. After all, "*some people spend a tremendous amount of energy merely to be normal*", quoted Lawrence to Layla.

"Layla. I am on my way to rehearsal, I am so lost in my mind - I am mentally rehearsing right now, that I did not realize it was you. Would you like some wine? You could come and hear the music from the backstage... Daniel is not in this band; this is way too experimental for him..."

Lawrence led the way, as Layla followed him inside the club. Lawrence introduced her to those who didn't know her. People Layla had never seen before were staring at her.

"She is family," he said, knowing people were investigating her, while he was tuning the piano.

Lawrence's talent echoed loudly in the room. Layla was halfway through with her glass of wine when the concert ended. She was always a slow drinker. Specifically with wine. She adored it, and there was no reason to rush.

Lawrence invited her to sit outside. The sky was a blue filled with hope.

"I think I should go and visit my wife, Anne, next month. I haven't seen her in five years."

He got out of his pocket a picture of her, Anne, and one of their kids, Catherine. In the photograph, Anne is wearing a long blue dress, and she is standing by the kitchen window while holding an extremely young Catherine in her arms. The sunlight hit Anne's wavy red hair. Catherine is staring into the camera.

"Those beautiful red hair, she still has them. I have some spies that tell me about her once or twice every year."

"*What a beautiful woman,*" said Layla, genuinely mesmerized.

"My wife is the strongest woman I know. I love her. We are still married, and I can feel her closer to me than everybody else, despite the distance. She probably had a few lovers during the recent years, I hope she did. That would never change what we had in any way. Oh, to love someone so truly that you want them happy, whether with you or without. To love someone enough to be aware that they're happier without you."

"I sincerely admire your affection. I do not think I am capable of that. I think that when I love someone, I want it to consume me. I want my person to be

mine. I need to be with them and around them." Layla was surprised by how much she felt comfortable sharing with Lawrence.

"You think that I would rather not be with her? I think about her always. That lady has never left my mind or my heart ever since I first glanced at her at a party decades ago. We were so young. How I would like it for her to be with me always."

"Why are you not?" asked Layla, perhaps a bit too daringly.

Lawrence took a sip from his wine glass and started talking while looking up, somewhere in the sky, or somewhere in his head.

"I haven't seen her because I have been an addict. I have a beautiful wife, and three kids, and all I was to them was a drug user. I am way luckier than anyone I grew up with, and I have been an addict. I will never wash it away. All the pain I caused. To everyone. To myself, even. I thought that one day, my kids would have understood. I thought that my wife would have understood. She was always on my side. My kids will never forgive me, and I do not blame them, for only I am to blame. I just wish they understood what it was like for me. I had no way of controlling my mind. I felt everything so deeply, and I was living inside my thoughts. I needed an escape. I needed a sort of… jazz, inside my head."

Lawrence turned to Layla, as she sat in silence, unsure of what to say. He wanted her to know him, though he didn't know why. He then decided to fully open up to Layla.

"One evening, I had too much of too much. My daughter, Catherine, found me. Anne loved classical music, and we used to collect LPs. A record by Vivaldi was playing in the room. Catherine was twelve."

Layla didn't know if she was closer to empathy or rage. She once knew someone who was an addict, too. She knew it wasn't right to compare experiences, but she just couldn't help it. She definitely wasn't going to forgive *that* addict in her life. That is because she only ever knew that woman as an addict. It was just like Lawrence said. An addict is all that woman was to her, despite the opportunity to be many things. She could have been a mother, since she did, in fact, give birth to a child. She was once a child herself. She was once a young woman with dreams to pursue. Layla found *that woman*'s diaries from when *the woman* was sixteen. Judging from the pictures and the notes, that woman had a boyfriend who loved running and playing the guitar with his friends. She was seriously interested in fashion and had multiple sketches of clothes that Layla would've loved to wear. She did not seem depressed at all. What Layla could never forgive wasn't the fact that the woman who gave birth to her was an addict; it was the fact that Layla was never given the opportunity to know her as anything else. If only Layla could have met *that woman,* the one she was before she was pregnant with her.

"I apologize. I hope this is not too much for you to bear. Somehow, you remind me of her, my daughter Catherine. She hasn't spoken to me in years, and, as you can perhaps imagine, she has her reasons. Sometimes, my spies tell me about her, too. She is still in New York, she is a good kid, and she is pursuing a degree in medicine. I wanted to send her money to help her pay for college, but Catherine wouldn't let me. She is disgusted by me. Don't misunderstand me, it's not that she was disgusted because I was violent. I never hit her or her mom; I was not that kind. I was the kind that disappeared and came back when at my lowest. I tried my best not to get violent in front of them. Her brother pities me; that is why he still calls. He is an environmental activist and a surfer; he moved somewhere on the East Coast, and he seems satisfied with his life. I have another daughter, too. She lives with her aunt, and they travel together a lot. I saw her recently. She asked me for tips for playing the piano after we hadn't talked for a few

years. That is all she could bear about me. A pianist. Not a junkie. I am still glad she reached out, obviously. I love that kid. I love all of my children."

"I am sorry," confessed Layla, sincerely.

"Every time that I play, I like to imagine my family in the crowd. The last time they heard me playing, my kids were not even ten. I used to picture Catherine in the spot that you usually sit on, back at the jazz bar. No one ever picks that chair because it's dark, and it's right in front of the door. People who sit there hate it when someone opens the door; they say it's cold. Anyway, that was until you came. It was like seeing her again, though I am aware you are Layla and not Catherine. It doesn't make me sad."

"It doesn't make you sad," repeated Layla out loud, undecided on how to process that comment.

"I apologize if I spoke too much," declared Lawrence, in a serious tone.

Layla thought that she also felt, at times, that she spoke too much. That feeling is isolated, and she didn't want to make Lawrence think he couldn't speak to her.

"You are my friend, Lawrence. I will always be here for your stories. I am grateful for every side of you I get to know, but I must go now. I need to pick up something in a bookstore that closes in twenty minutes."

"See you, Layla. Sometimes, it feels good to be seen off-stage, even if that is not our favorite version," said Lawrence. Layla walked and walked and walked. She stopped on the way to take some photographs. The sky was darker and clearer now: the weather was changing. By the time she got to her destination, the bookstore was closed. She sat on the steps of the shop's entrance and lit a cigarette. She thought of Lawrence's recent words. Being someone off-stage. The version of ourselves we hide, the one we lock in the most exclusive backstage. The rawest jam we play.

Chapter V.

Hello, Anne (A Love Supreme)

As Layla sat still in her usual spot, Daniel, Lawrence, and the rest were playing.
Layla had this thing that she addressed as *"giving life to the camera aperture,"* which consisted of putting a hand in front of her eyes, forming an O with her finger, and obscuring everything except for something specific, to allow herself to look at nothing but that particular thing. She would often do it with Daniel. It was part of her inspiration. As she drew, Layla wondered whether she kept going to the jazz club to belong somewhere, to be a part of something. She wanted these artists, whom she dedicated most of her nights to, to pronounce her name as soon as she entered. She wanted Lawrence to share more of his memories with her.
She wanted Daniel to come and *"bother her"*, as he would say.
One thing was clear: Layla was going to spend the whole night up listening to Billie Holiday. A woman in her sixties with beautiful red hair,

wearing an elegant blue dress and a white fur coat, entered the jazz bar. To Layla, it was clear from the start who that woman was. As he noticed her, Lawrence abruptly stopped playing. All eyes were on the elegant woman as she turned her back and opened the door to leave, soon after arriving. Instead of running after his wife, Lawrence slowly went up to the bar and asked for some whiskey. The band tried to keep going on without a pianist. Layla ran up to Lawrence, leaving her stuff unattended.

"Are you seriously not going to run after her?" she asked.
Lawrence took a sip of whiskey, staring at the void, somewhere in front of his very own eyes.
Layla shook her head. *"You can do better than that."*
She went out of the club, rushing after Lawrence's wife.
"Lawrence mentions you very often, madame," yelled Layla, trying to catch her.
The elegant woman stopped.
"I highly doubt it," she said in a neutral, honest tone. Layla turned her back. Lawrence began to

follow them, doing his best to be as silent as possible.
"I mean it, Anne," Layla told her, as she finally reached her.
Anne stopped and turned her back to face Layla.
"You really do look like someone I know," said Anne. She analysed Layla's figure from head to toe.
Anne caught Layla's eyes, only to break eye contact at the sight of Lawrence getting nearer.
Layla smiled. *"I will leave you guys to it."*
The woman in the fur coat took a cigarette out of her bag. As she looked for the lighter, Lawrence reached Anne. He always had a lighter in his pocket, so he handed it to her.
"She looks just like Catherine, I know. She even has her sense of humor, I assure you. It's pure madness." he took a loud, deep breath and said, *"Hello, Anne."*
Layla went back to her drawings. Lawrence and Anne went back to a sense of familiarity only they could provide to each other.
Anne did not have another lover after Lawrence; no matter how much time passed, her feelings, though hurt, were the same.

At the end of the set, Layla realized she had spent the entire evening drawing Anne.
Layla and Daniel decided to head back to Daniel's place with the red Vespa that night.
"Who was that?" asked Daniel, on the scooter.
"That was Lawrence's wife, her name is Anne," answered Layla, loud enough for Daniel to hear.
Daniel then worried whether he posed an obvious question. He then decided it was only fair to ask. He thought about Lawrence and Layla getting closer than he and Lawrence were. He liked that.
"Lawrence never listens to me, but he always listens to you. I wonder why that is. The other day, we had to restart the jam three times for him to agree that the piano wasn't loud enough. Insomma (one of the few Italian words Daniel knew, which he adored, accompanied by a fake Italian accent), one would think that he is behaving that way because of his age, but no! He just won't listen, he never did!"
expressed Daniel, once off the Vespa.
"I think that might be because I remind him of his daughter." A moment of silence followed.
"... I care for him, truly."
Before that moment, Daniel never thought about how present Layla was in his life and

routine. He put his arm around her shoulder as they went up to his apartment.

The day after, when Layla got back home, she met a neighbor on the stairs, watering some plants. He was quite an old man. He was wearing a pair of rain boots and denim overalls, and he seemed to put a lot of care into the plants.

"I found these at the trash station, in the corner," said the man, turning to Layla. *"Non ci crederesti a quante di queste creature di Dio vengono buttate ogni giorno. Io provo a salvarle. / You wouldn't believe how many beautiful creatures of God get thrown there every day. I am trying to save them."*

"I would like to help you! I live on the first floor. If you'd ever like some help, you can come look for me," said Layla as she walked up the stairs. From her window, Layla stared at the moon the same way someone who is seeking answers stares at the sky. She wondered about the perception of different things. Humans, plants, wars, relationships, death, addiction, and blood. They must have had something in common; after all, they were all simultaneously real on the same rock.

Layla was once again alone. She put a record on and cleaned up her studio a little bit. She thought of Anne, and she thought of Lawrence. She hoped Anne and Lawrence would soon take care of some plants together again. Then she thought of Daniel. She imagined herself and Daniel growing old together, as their plants multiplied, died, and came back to life. They could get a small, old apartment and paint the walls red. It wouldn't be in Rome. It would be somewhere else, perhaps somewhere in the South. Music would be present in each room, at all times, and together they would have a quite good record collection. Daniel knows how to bake better than Layla, and he could teach her. They could learn to knit together and give each other handmade sweaters. She could reveal to him her best Italian recipes. She could stare at him with a humble regard after getting the entire kitchen dirty just to attempt the perfect tiramisu. It would be a life filled with laughter. It would be quite a life.

Chapter VI.
A Sunday for the mind (Giant Steps).

If Layla stopped to take a picture now, it would be difficult to tell the season from the image. Southern Europe was great at playing that game. Layla looked at the time: she was three hours early to work, so she decided to go for a walk in the park. She sat under a tree, she had a book in her hands, and the sun was touching her face. She then delicately closed her eyes and took a deep breath. Her headphones were transmitting John Coltrane. She thought that Sunday could be her day. Growing up, Sunday was the day she feared the most. Richard was off work on Sundays, and every week, they would begin to argue before lunchtime, hence they'd have to spend the day in their rooms trying not to engage too much with each other and avoid a second fight. Layla would often cry at the dining table. Richard would then yell at her until he fell asleep with his head on the table. It was torturous.

The thought of Sundays also reminded her of a story Lawrence had recently told her. Back to a couple of years before he went to live with Trevor and Leo, he fell in love with the piano. He had told Layla that story after she asked why, out of all things, Lawrence, a young boy without a roof over his head, asked Angela for a piano. On a spring day, he had found an MP3 in Central Park, and he decided to keep it. He didn't have any headphones, so he went and stole a cheap pair from a big electronics store. When he finally put them in the MP3, that's when his ears first met McCoy Tyner. A few days passed, and listening to McCoy quickly became Lawrence's favorite part of the day. That motivated him to keep waking up each day and looking for something to eat. The motivation for him to seek some rest at night was thinking about when he would listen again to his American composer's delicate touch. One day, while he was strolling around, he spotted an old piano through an open door. He decided to head in. The place was empty, and the piano was gently covered by a blanket of dust. It was a Sunday. He was uncertain at first, afraid of both being noticed by someone and the subsequent possibility of never getting the chance to play again. He started by playing an easy riff, D E F

G, over and over again. After a couple of hours, he decided to look for some music sheets to read and analyze. He would have tried to come back the next Sunday and see if the door was still open. In the meantime, he got some sheets from a local library. The Sunday afterward, he managed to get in again, and, strangely, he felt a calling somewhere inside of him that told him to get closer to the piano - up to this moment, Lawrence was the kind of person who would get bored with anything right after trying and not being a master at it right away. The piano taught him how to be patient, and, somehow, how to be kinder to himself, too.

While navigating these thoughts, Layla felt blue. She had a good day, and nothing particularly bad happened. Not in her life, at least. She went to the library with Alex, and then she spent the evening taking self-portraits. There was nothing that could explain her sudden change of humor. It was like there were different versions of her that she would put on like clothes, leave on the side (or on a messy chair somewhere in her room), and eventually pick back up. They weren't necessarily masks; they were pure yet unpredictable and often difficult to deal with. Both for Layla and the people in her life. Layla often dreamt of moving to the edge of society, close to nature and nature only. That way, perhaps her mind would be a calmer place to live in. A real Sunday for the mind. She liked being on her own. Somehow, it made her feel more real, to be disconnected. There were moments in which she felt as if she was incapable of truly liking anyone at all - eventually, everyone became annoying, or perhaps they were nice, but then she had to spend her days trying not to be misunderstood. At times, Layla would lie on the grass, regardless of the weather, and fantasize about murdering someone evil and then running away. The next step would be moving into a house close to the water, but far from boats and overcrowded beaches with noisy children. But then again, could she ever be a murderer? She was kind, wasn't she? Perhaps it was exactly the hate she felt raging inside of her that led her to her kindness.

Later that day, Layla was physically at work, but mentally somewhere unknown. They were yelling something about sparkling water with not enough bubbles as she was playing a song in her head. She was always thinking about someone, uncertain whether these people themselves would also spend so much time in their head or not. Layla thought about Daniel and what he did when he wasn't playing a jam or practicing. She knew he enjoyed reading other musicians' biographies. She yearned to know what he would usually get at the supermarket, or if he ever practiced any sport when he was younger.

Did Lawrence tell Daniel about his conversation with Layla?

She could have asked, she could have called. Layla thought of Alex, too. The two could go for days without talking to each other. Sometimes, Layla felt very interested in discovering the version of Alex that he was when completely alone, the version of himself that only he could ever know. It felt like her own best friend was a stranger, too, behind the mask that was her own presence. Layla looked at the clock. One last hour, and she could begin to close the restaurant, the endless task of her job. As she carried the plates, she fantasized about leaving the city. She then opened her phone and saw that there was a flight to England for nine pounds the following week. London could be good, and she had a few days off. A customer broke a wine glass by mistake. As Layla stood motionless near the mess, she could perceive the eyes of her colleagues on her, as well as the customers'. A colleague told her to move fast and that she was impossible to understand. She thought her colleagues were also impossible to understand, but there was a difference between the two sides. They were all the same in her eyes, and she was standing alone in their eyes. There were no bad feelings about it.

After all, Layla was convinced that one has a little life when they don't let their feelings live, and she never witnessed any of her colleagues showing any particular emotion. They were there exclusively to repeat tasks mechanically, in an exploitative loop. Work must include alienation; this was pretty evident, and definitely not the workers' fault, yet, appearing a little bit more human wouldn't go to waste, according to Layla. Luckily, she wasn't too good at it, and she cried at the restaurant once or twice. Something Layla truly enjoyed about her job was overhearing the conversations of the customers. She would often end up visualizing their personalities against their will and make up full backstories about them in her head. More than a waitress, she was mentally a screenwriter, and the customers were nothing but her characters. The clock. It was time to check out and go home. Layla tried to call Alex, but he didn't pick up. It was a warm evening in September in Rome, and she had no intention of going straight to bed. She considered texting Daniel, but in the end, she chose not to. Perhaps she should've put more effort into building new relationships. There were so many women she wished she could be closer to, but none of them were close enough for Layla to call in the evening and plan a hangout at the last minute. She had one childhood friend from her hometown, whom she met before she even learned how to read, Cara. They were still close, but they didn't text or call much. The two ladies had a similar childhood, a shared passion for art, a common music taste, and a lot of weaknesses and strengths to discuss. Layla always thought of Cara as a sister.

Neither of them would usually call the other while in need of help, but that didn't stop them from always being there for each other. Layla briefly considered inviting Cara to go to London with her. Despite Cara being her realest and longest friendship, they never went on a trip together. Layla would usually travel alone. It was flexible and cheap, and it provided personal growth. It could also get lonely, but it wasn't the kind of loneliness she would mind. As long as it inspired her.

No. No. No. It wasn't good. Layla was about to feel inescapably sad again. She could feel it. What could she do? She had to do something. She didn't have much money. It was already 11 p.m. Boredom and guilt always assaulted her simultaneously. Layla felt guilty for feeling bored, and bored by feeling guilty for it. She hoped an old friend would reach out. Maybe Cara. Cara wouldn't save her; nobody could, but it would be nice to feel her close again. Layla and Cara had clicked instantly in kindergarten. Cara had just moved to Italy from Ireland when school started, and she didn't know any Italian. Layla wasn't fluent in English then, as Richard always spoke Italian inside the house. Their fast connection might have something to do with the fact that, between them, the language barrier didn't matter. They felt distant from everybody else, together. They understood each other so deeply that the other kids felt intimidated by them. Now, they would call or meet barely once or twice every year, but, as time went by, they stayed close, despite life and growing up. The love was always there; Layla knew that, and Cara knew that too. There was a video on Layla's phone of Cara and her running after each other all over the school's courtyard. Neither of them was capable of watching it without bursting into tears. So many people have left since then. So many things happened. The video was recorded on Cara's birthday. Layla suddenly revisited a lot of their memories together, inside her mind. They both saw the other going insane. They truly saw the other, growing into one person and then another. Too much xanax. Too much cake. Too much love. Too much vomit. Not enough. Too much weight. Too many expectations. Too much of the unshareable, to share. Not enough change. Not enough actions. Too many people leaving the -

at times poetic, at times pathetic - show. Not enough people in the backstage. Too much importance was given to numbers. Too little quality was given to their relationships.
Layla went back to her studio and decided that re-arranging it for the fifth time might turn it into "her place". At first, she considered painting it, but she didn't know how long she was going to stay there, and it could have turned into a big expense. She then contemplated inverting the desk and the bookshelf, but she had to move the wardrobe first. Layla then began to throw her clothes on the floor and carefully piled up books in her kitchen corner. One hour went by. It was typical of her to believe that the place of her furniture would change the place of her mind in some way. She would obsess over the arrangement for hours, then forget it ever happened for weeks or months, just to finally feel the urge to change it all over again. Who knows, maybe something could, in fact, change by changing the order or the furniture. A red curtain instead of a blue one. A poster from the Nouvelle Vague. A scented candle. A smaller drawer. As it often happened during these kinds of evenings, Layla

fell asleep with her desk in the middle of the room and her possessions all over the place. When she woke up, she thought that, if she saw a photograph of herself in that position, she would finally think of that studio as "her place." Peacefully sleeping amid the chaos that she provided for herself.

Chapter VII.
Layla's birthday (Ghost of Yesterday)

It was Layla's 21st Birthday. It was also a busy Friday for everyone. Now that high school was a distant memory, she had to look for fresh ways to entertain herself. She didn't tell Daniel it was her birthday, and he had a concert scheduled that night. Alex was off to a film festival in Paris with his mom.

That morning, Layla decided to read a book she had on her shelf and had never read before. Shortly after, unable to pay proper attention to the words she was holding in her hands, Layla went to the nearest pasticceria to get a chocolate cupcake, unaware of how to spend the rest of the day. She put a bow around the cupcake's paper and a small Post-it with the text "happy birthday, Lay" and left a kiss mark on it.

An unknown number called.

It was Lawrence.

"Hello, Layla. Lawrence here. Am I bothering you? I saw online that it's your birthday today. It's my birthday, as well. I have a small present for you, and I truly hope you don't mind. I am guessing you are partying today, but we could meet over a coffee

sometime soon, or I could bring it to the jazz club later if you're coming."

"Lawrence, hi," she said, looking at the clock. It was already noon. She hadn't even drunk any coffee yet. *"How does 2 p.m. sound to you?"*

Just like she liked it, Layla got ready in a rush and got out of the house fast. There was no time to think. Lawrence was waiting for her.

He suggested they'd meet at a cafe in Monti, where he used to work when he first arrived in Rome. The atmosphere was friendly and calm, and pigeons were flying all over the square. He then took out from his backpack a vinyl of Derek and the Dominos, "Layla And Other Assorted Love Songs".

"I thought you might like this," affirmed Lawrence.

She did.

"Thank you. You know, my name actually comes from one of my favorite songs. Layla. I found out by chance, a long, long time ago."

Layla looked outside the window. It started to rain. She felt slightly ashamed for not knowing it was Lawrence's birthday too, since he somehow found out that it was hers.

"I always liked that song. I used to sing it with Anne in the car. Some of the sweetest air I consumed next to her, I consumed while singing along to that song. I

hope she remembers it, the same way I do," said Lawrence.

"I am sure she does," boldly stated Layla.

"What age are you celebrating today?" she then asked.

"Sixty-three years of rain and shine," declared Lawrence, with a smile on his face.

"I don't intend to steal too much of your time. You are young and full of life; you should go have fun. You should go sing along. I hope to see you at the jam later. And tell that stronzo of Daniel that today is your day. Please."

"I have a little sweet treat for you," said Layla, while handing him a chocolate cupcake she had bought that morning, right after getting one for herself. *"Happy birthday, Lawrence"*.

He took the present and farewelled the young lady with a smile on his face.

When he left, Layla seemed relieved, to some extent. She was glad to have Lawrence in her life.

Inspired by that spontaneous meeting, she decided to stay in the cafe and draw some sketches. She drew what she aspired to look like once she'd reached Lawrence's age. A lovely, kind old lady with a bob haircut that turned gray. In the drawing, she is wearing a huge jumper she made herself. She is not scared anymore, and she still feels deeply. She wasted too much time in her youth feeling hate and rage, and she is as patient and gentle as ever.

Layla then headed back home, as she kept fantasizing about being old. On the bus, she spotted a lady with a well-cured and grey bob haircut. She didn't look anything like Layla: she had blue eyes, she was wearing sweatpants, and she was quite tall and skinny. Layla deliberately ignored the lack of similarities and interpreted it as a sign that she would, one day, grow old and gentle and gently old. Once closer to her apartment, she opened her letterbox, where she found a letter from Alex.

It was a letter with quite a childish drawing of a red heart with the text *"Joyeux anniversaire, tuo, Alex."*

Perhaps, at the end of the day, love was real. She put on her favorite shoes and headed to the jazz bar. As soon as she entered, the bartender gave her a glass of wine. *"It's on the band,"* he said. Layla knew it was from Lawrence. She hadn't eaten anything since the cupcake, and, as

a consequence, she became mildly inebriated after drinking that one glass.
Daniel came and held her.
"Happy birthday, Lay," he whispered as he leaned in and offered his cheek for Layla to kiss, as a way of greeting her. He did it quite often, ever since Layla once told him that it was *"an Italian thing".* Daniel thought the Italian way of greeting people really said a lot about Italian culture. The jam was on, and they played a jazz cover of "Layla". While she was once again drowning in jazz, she wondered what it was, exactly, that made people feel happy to be somewhere. She concluded that it was other people. It's always about the people. A vague sense of shame related to letting other people dictate her feelings persuaded her, but she couldn't help it. She was a lover.
"It's Lawrence's birthday, too, today!" she yelled, between a song and the next. The band then took a short break to hug Lawrence, and that's when Layla knew what she wanted: to belong somewhere, like they all seemed to do. In the same way, she forgot how sick in her head she was feeling the day before; she feared she would soon forget how warm her birthday felt.

Once Layla came back to her studio, she looked around herself. The place was small but welcoming. Scented candles and incense were never lacking, and there was always a record, a book, or both to keep her company. There were clothes gathered on a specific chair on a daily basis, and there were always dirty cups in the sink. It was really such a pity that the contract wasn't long enough for her to paint the walls. Technically, she wasn't even allowed to hang stuff on the walls, but she did it anyway.

"Oh, please spare me. I will ask for some extra shifts, and I will pay back the damage. They wouldn't give me my deposit back anyway", Layla once told Alex when, preoccupied, he entered her apartment, and he *"felt assaulted by the amount of stuff hung on the walls"*.

Layla knew that the day she would buy an apartment would come. A small and cozy home that would be developed over two floors. On the ground floor, a living room - not too big, yet big enough for a record player and a bar corner. The living room would be colored burgundy-red wine, and it would turn into a jazz club at least once a week. The thought of being able to host jazz jams in her home someday kept her going. She would get a giant painting by an unknown artist met during some trip somewhere and hang it in her bedroom, upstairs. Her bed would lie in a room dedicated entirely to art, which she would fill with her own creativity as well as other people's productions. Last but not least, she really wanted a red fridge. How superficial, how lovely.

Layla's phone was suddenly full of light.

"I didn't forget your birthday, I swear, Lay, it is not midnight yet. I am downstairs. You better be home, alone, and awake." Layla and Cara hadn't met in months, perhaps, even a year. She opened the door.

Layla was certainly not in her prime, although seeing Cara's face made her want to bake. They improvised a vegan carrot cake, then they watched a movie.

"Hiroshima Mon Amour has to be one of my favorites," Layla told Cara.

"Clearly," her friend replied.

The two friends proceeded to do nothing together.

Their silence was never flustering, and never empty. Cara wanted to tell Layla that she missed her, though she knew she would end up making useless old promises about visiting her more often. It wasn't like Layla would ever step foot into her hometown. She couldn't bring herself to do it; she got sick at the thought. She wouldn't even think of it as her hometown but rather as a place she once knew and shall never again. Cara and Layla went out for a smoke.

"I think I might be allergic to gluten," said Cara.
"That sounds awful. I hope you are wrong."
Cara looked at Layla with complicity.
"Do you remember that old yellow puppet you used to have?" Cara asked.
"Mister Chop! How could I ever forget!" stated Layla.
"Where the hell is he?" asked Cara.
"I must have lost it while moving places, I think," admitted Layla, vaguely ashamed for not knowing.
"THAT would be awful," replied Cara.
"...Yet not as awful as you being allergic to gluten," concluded Layla.

Cara stayed with Layla for a couple of days. They got along quite well as roommates; they even kept joking about moving in together somewhere far away someday. Cara always wanted to move to the north of Italy and have a small house filled with cats and a postbox of letters that Layla would fill.

"Cara, I met someone," Layla told Cara, on their second day together.
"Don't I know it? The jazz guy?"
Cara passed Layla a joint she rolled and mixed with lavender.
Cara was glad to see Layla appearing less embarrassed about being human than she had been before.
"You know, for most of my life, I thought that trauma was all I knew. All I could relate to. All there was to bond on. Recently, though, there are times - they are rare, but they are there - in which I could really imagine a future, a future that isn't based on my past," said Cara.
Layla understood what Cara meant, though she wasn't sure she could relate.
"Although I never text or call - except this very particular time, I want you to know that I think about you constantly. I look at the photographs you

take, and I feel amazed. The picture you recently took of people crossing the street... it makes me think about the future. All these people walking in different directions, different clothes, different classes, different dreams, different ideas... Something about it fascinates me and frightens me at the same time," revealed Cara.

They rolled a second joint.

"I believe that the privilege of not knowing what you are going to be, consume, and create is incomparable, though I can't deny how scared I am. I have no interest in any particular career, and money disgusts me - though I could use a bit of it. Do you have any idea how you intend to spend the rest of your life? Does anyone have a clue about what we are all doing?" asked Layla.

"We should hunt down whoever decided humans should live off anything that isn't natural," suggested Cara.

"We'll get there, you'll lead a revolution someday," concluded Layla, feeling hopeless and inspired at the same time.

Cara left the next morning and, as she was outside Layla's building waiting for the bus, she looked up and wondered when they would meet again and who they would be then.

Chapter VIII.
A slow and unsurprising death on a rainy day (Autumn Leaves)

It was evident, Jazz had become Layla's biggest inspiration for her photography. Layla became interested in photography at a very young age, ever since she realized that everything comes to an end, eventually. The opportunity to get a moment to be stuck forever felt powerful. One of Layla's biggest fears was losing her memory someday. A clean state: something to fear and to yearn for at the same time. Richard gave Layla her first camera when she turned six. The oldest picture she shot was a photo of an autumn leaf captured during a hike with Richard. She didn't want to let it go, and after photographing it, she took it home and hung it on their fridge. That leaf stayed with them for months, lying between the pages of a young Layla's diary until it disintegrated.

That evening, Layla was late to the jazz bar. She rushed there. An old lady approached her and asked if it was her that she had heard screaming the night before, in the middle of the bar. Layla was sweating, and she did not remember.

Usually, the concert would go as follows: Layla would open the window and subsequently get Lawrence mad - he loved suffering the warmth of the Italian city and the candles, then she would order some red wine to sip while absorbing the music from the table in front of the door. Lawrence and Daniel would usually go and talk to her between breaks, and afterwards they'd stop for a drink with Layla and the band after the concert. They would all stay there and talk about whatever until the jazz bar would have to close, typically at around 1 a.m., and the bartender would send Daniel, Layla, Lawrence, and everybody else away.

This time, Lawrence was not there. Who was there, however, was Alex. For the very first time. He wanted to try it and see for himself why Layla loved it so much. During the break, Alex told Layla that he could not see what she saw in Jazz. He thought it was too chaotic, and he hated the thought of not being in control of it. If Alex were a music genre, it would be classical music. He then proceeded to ask questions. Asking questions was Alex's specialty.

"Why have you been drawing while they are playing?" asked Alex.

"Alex, all the wine in the world won't make you capable of reading me. It is not your fault," stated Layla.

She was still sweating, and she felt disgusting. Her thoughts were foggy.

Suddenly, a note was played that tasted like a shooting star. That was a jazz jam to Layla, a chase between stars.

"It's as if humans had fingers exclusively to make art," Layla told Alex.

"Un grande castello. I want a big castle, somewhere here in Italy, and I want to dance inside it and compose music on a piano. An old friend is going to be there, somewhere, and he's going to play for me in my sleep. I also want a lake, and I want to swim in it, and still compose. Nothing else matters in the world if not art. Don't misunderstand me, being human is art too, or at least it was, or maybe it is until we leave, and perhaps good artists never leave…"

"What?" said Alex, who didn't get a word of what Layla was telling him, because the trumpet was too loud. He then told his friend:

"I am going home. I've got a lot on my plate planned for tomorrow. I have to wake up early to go to a premiere. I hope you have a nice time, despite my absence," and left.

Daniel was also running late that night, and he joined the jam during the very last set. He came in rapidly and got his saxophone out straight away. Something about Daniel was different. He wasn't looking at Layla the way he usually would, and he didn't even bother saying *"hello"* to the bartender.

Layla looked at Daniel. A part of her wanted to believe there could be something real between them, but a stronger part of her felt she was too obscure for him. Once, the two were walking in Trastevere when Daniel said, entirely out of the *blues*, *"I think you are obsessed with death"*.

As she immersed herself in that memory, a whispered *"there's no escape"* came out of her mouth. The music was still on. Sometimes, Layla would feel so lost in the jazz that she was incapable of getting out. It was a double-sided quality.

Daniel finished his set, finally acknowledged the presence of the bartender, and sat next to Layla with a beer.

A familiar face from the Jazz bar came, placed her hand on Daniel's shoulder, and said, *"I am very sorry for your loss, dear."*

Daniel smiled like he would when something bothered him: he would briefly show his teeth, curve his head towards his right shoulder, and close his eyes. He then turned to Layla.

That night was coming to an end earlier than the Sun was planning to rise. Birds were not to be heard anywhere, and the wind that moved the plants all over the city was no longer loud. Layla and Daniel took the Vespa and went back to Daniel's place. Layla opened the window as soon as she entered, just like she would do at the jazz bar. The last time she opened a window at the jazz bar, just a few days before, Lawrence was there too. She then recalled the time Lawrence told her that he appreciated her willingness to open the window, despite Layla's aim to bother him, for that meant she noticed people and things around her.

— —

Lawrence passed away earlier that week. It was a slow and unsurprising death on a rainy day. Daniel and Layla went together to the funeral, where they didn't exchange a single word. The silence was deafening enough.
Daniel was now drowning on his sofa, nervously passing his hands through his hair. The sofa was in the left corner by the window, where Layla was standing.

Lawrence was addicted to many things, but it wasn't that kind of withdrawal that killed him. It was Anne. *"They never invented a rehab to get over people, and perhaps they should,"* he once told Layla.

Lawrence died precisely one month after meeting Anne. That was a deadly coincidence to Anne, who usually did not believe in such things as coincidences. Although she did not earn herself a grave, she stopped eating and taking care of herself. It was because of Anne's depression that Catherine found out Lawrence was dead. No one would dare tell her. In the past, when Catherine was younger, and an uncle or an auntie or whatever kind of relative would dare mention Lawrence's name to her, she would go insane. *"You don't know the Lawrence I know, and I do not know the Lawrence you knew, and he is the one to blame. Now shut up, or I swear I will burn the entire house down and you will never see me again."*

Anne consumed the last proper meal two days before Lawrence's death. Just like she knew. *"the body…"*, said Anne to Catherine, *"…it's like, like it has a sixth sense… like my body gets to know certain things before I do."*

"Sure, Mom, but now, please, eat," would reply Catherine, exhausted.

Unsure of how to deal with yet another end, Layla suggested playing chess. Daniel took the small set of chess he used to carry in his bag, set it, and placed it on the table, gently inviting Layla to make the first move with a gesture. They both managed a quite banal opening while avoiding each other's eyes.
Quietly, she finally looked at him and asked,
"What are we doing?"
Since Lawrence died, Daniel's eyes seemed to have absorbed the white nothingness of the snow. An outrageous silence was now expanding in the room. Daniel opened his mouth, intending to eject his voice, but something stopped him.
"You have known Lawrence for ages. I am here for you, I am your friend," Layla murmured.
An inconsistent amount of seconds went by.
Irrevocably, Daniel opened up: *"He never even learned Italian. He was buried in a language that wasn't his own. That priest didn't even speak English, and Lawrence wasn't even Christian. What if that happened to me? What if I had to be buried in a language I do not speak?"*

"Lawrence died at the age of sixty-seven. You are not even twenty-five. He died calmly, and he made art until his very last day," Layla took a deep breath. *"Lawrence wouldn't make it a tragedy. We loved him, he was loved, he is loved. I hope that, if he is somewhere, he is proud of who he was."*

"He was so kind," replied Daniel.

"I know," remarked Layla.

"He wouldn't usually get paid much; he was often struggling to pay rent, and yet he would still donate a significant part of his salary to the local charity."

"I know," remarked Layla, insensible to her own tears.

"He was the kind of person who would pay for the coffee of the first customer waiting in line at a cafe with not enough cash on their hand, while everyone else would just be annoyed for such a waste of time."

"I know."

"He loved street musicians - he has been one too, but you know. He was more than that. More than anything we could ever say. He was just good to be around. That doesn't happen with many people."

Layla looked at Daniel, yearning for a way to embrace his inner being.

"I understand," she said.

Layla sat next to Daniel. The painting by Malcolm T. Liepke she had hung in her kitchen now resembled Daniel in Layla's arms. He cried.

The rain slowly started falling for the first time after Lawrence's death. The first time after a Death. That is what they both needed.
The sound of the rain was growing louder every second, as Daniel lay on her, and she kept playing with his hair.

"Layla, I want to move back to New York," whispered Daniel.

Layla couldn't bring herself to even think of an answer. She kept placing her finger between his hair, and she eventually touched his face, almost as if she needed to memorise it, in silence. Eventually, once the rain calmed down, she stood up, grabbed her coat, and left. Nervously waiting to get back to her studio and melt.

Chapter IX.
To let it happen is to die (Straight, No Chaser)

Layla was unsure of the reason why she got a ticket to London. The destination of her journey was completely irrelevant. She did not book a place to spend the night, and she ended up in a hostel behind Trafalgar Square. She couldn't even remember how she got there. She looked at her stuff. It was cold outside, and she didn't bring anything that was properly adequate to the British weather. She put on a scarf and went for a walk. She was sick of her own mind. If only she could be someone else, just for a while...

All she needed was a place to go, somewhere that would call for her, somewhere to belong to. Somewhere to be understood. Layla had nowhere to go back to, and she worked and worked and worked to make her own, but it seemed like her efforts weren't enough. There was always something that she couldn't bring herself to reach.

A cozy bar in a rather dark street disrupted her thoughts. A jazz jam was on. As Layla took advantage of the break to come in and take a seat, all she could see were ghosts. Empty places that were never meant to be filled again. Daniel was gone, Lawrence was dead. She stared at the piano immeuble, in silence, long enough for the bartender to come and ask her if she was all right. Layla smiled at her, but she couldn't bring herself to say anything. It didn't cost her much effort to project Lawrence's fingers and the music that came out of them. Her face had to be wet for Layla to realize she was crying. Tears were not the only ones coming for her; she could feel the vomit coming, too. She puked in the jazz bar's restroom. Just as if that jazz bar's restroom was her own. Layla might as well be born on Mars, with a red body and a nose placed where a human's ears would belong. Where would the music enter a Martian's body from? Perhaps music would only be able to get out of them. A species that could finally stop the unwanted jam in their minds- or perhaps, it was all wrong. Maybe the Martians had the capacity of absorbing music entirely, physically and intensively, through every inch of their being.

Layla felt like an alien, as she kept throwing up and fantasizing about living on Mars. She stole a rose from a table, took a flyer, and headed out of the bar. It was the first and last time in her life that Layla walked out of the jazz bar before the music was over. She wasn't sure where to go next. The city that was already irrelevant was now a stranger. She sat on the sidewalk and started drawing all the good things that were inside the bar: the flowers, the instruments, the sound of people. The same things that made her nauseous. Someone was staring at her. A quite creepy yet somehow interesting Englishman was staring at her. He offered her some wine in exchange for some ears to listen to him bragging about Shakespeare.

Layla was bored. They headed back inside, where, as promised, he got a bottle of wine. "*Shakespeare wrote a lot,*" said the Englishman, justifying the bottle. Despite a brief dispute on whether Shakespeare's best play is Othello or Hamlet, they talked for hours, until the man offered Layla to stay with him for a few days. They were both aware it wasn't conventional, but

a. Layla wasn't that enthusiastic about staying in that hostel;
b. She had nothing to lose and nowhere to go.

They drank another bottle before heading to his place. Layla was genuinely surprised to find out that she had a whole bedroom for herself. The Englishman, who, according to the doorbell, was named Oscar, mentioned something about the University of Oxford.
"Oscar?," said Layla, uncertain of who she was calling from the corridor.
"Yes?" he replied.
"I have never been to Oxford, I'd like to," she mentioned in a confident tone that didn't belong to her. She had no genuine interest in such a place, and she was surprised to hear such words come out of her mouth.
"We can go tomorrow morning. Be up at 9," he concluded, before heading to his room.
Layla looked around the room. It was quite modern and minimalistic, and it lacked a personality. If she cared enough, she would despise it. But she didn't. She didn't care for anything anymore. There were no more

photographs to plan. No more music to be heard. The world was silent.

The next day, they took Oscar's car and went to Oxford. In the evening, they decided to turn it into a road trip. They drove between vintage bookstores for the following three days. Oscar insisted on playing Frank Sinatra in the car until Layla couldn't stand it anymore, and it grew on her so much that she asked to head back to London. The days spent together were delusional: at first, it was okay, but then she realized there weren't any more layers to peel off Oscar; that was all there was. Oscar's personality wasn't strong enough to be a distraction from her own destruction. It had nothing to do with him.

"Are you heading back to Rome?" he asked her, once back in London.

"I am heading home," she said.

"I have a feeling we'll meet again, someday," declared Oscar before taking Layla's black bag out of the car and handing it to her. She didn't take it.

Instead, she took a deep breath and ran. She rushed her way between people, memories, spaces, busy restaurants, tourists, lovers, photographs, music, and London. She ran all the way up to the closest bridge. One last dive. There were no substances nor morbid goodbyes. Not a single dream died there. She wasn't leaving anything incomplete.

Alex would never be able to read her; lord knows if there was anyone capable of reading her at all. On that cold Wednesday night in London, Layla took her last breath. Some might argue she took her last breath willingly, some would argue the opposite.

Whose decision is it, to decide to end it?

In the end, the answer doesn't matter. She jumped into the water the same way one jumps into a pool. The same way one jumps into life. Everything, everything is in motion. Constantly. Her way of dying was opposed to Lawrence's way; it was fast. It was alive.

During her last day, endless thoughts crossed her mind. She thought of Cara, her oldest friend. She thought of some she believed she hated. She thought of Daniel. She thought of Alex. She thought of her dad and that one picture she had found while moving houses. She thought of that giant turkey.

The end of life was just a place. It was the end of it. To worry so much, just to leave it as it happens. For some, to let it happen is to die. So many things were never going to happen. Layla would never grow old, nor see Richard grow older. She was now condemned to stay young forever. Alex would live his life without knowing much about the other characters in Layla's life. Her death turned his best friend into a stranger: Layla's last peel. She was someone who wanted to devour life, and she clung to that desire until her final push. People can die more than once. They're pulled away piece by piece until there is nothing left. Human beings can be consumed. Layla knew that and resisted it fiercely. Until she didn't anymore.

Chapter X.

That cake did nothing to you (Solitude)

"*You are the only one who comprehends me. No. You are the one who could understand me, but you don't. Can you please understand me? It is absurd. Everything is absurd. I don't even understand if you love me at all. I can't keep going this way. Loving you is harrowing. It's pathetic. Many are the labels I would joyfully use towards you: a friend, a husband, a father, a brother, a partner. Any kind of label that would imply a deeper connection. You could even be a cloud, flying above me, drunk with the assumption that you are not being noticed all the time. But I do. I notice everything you do. I just don't understand it. I can't comprehend what you want. What we have will kill me. The individualism I'm condemned to live with every day will kill me.*"

Alex never found the courage to open that letter until today. He had stolen it the day he read a piece on Layla's green notebook. The first thought that crossed his mind was that Layla would have laughed at her own letter if she read that now. He always suspected she wanted a little bit more from him, and now he knew she had been yearning for a deeper connection, with him, or with anyone.

The plane to London was calling. Alex thought about Layla's green notebook for the whole duration of the flight. A man in his fifties was sitting next to him, acting super busy on his Pc. Alex was almost sure that his seat neighbor was watching porn. Perhaps he was making it all up in his head, desperately trying to distract himself from any thought possibly related to Layla. Alex had rented an apartment near Bond Street. He had an appointment with a boy named Oscar that evening, and he was ready two hours earlier than he needed to, so he went for a walk. While walking, he came to the realization that he couldn't distract himself anymore. Everything reminded him of Layla. Alex did not go to Layla's funeral - it was probably not what she wanted anyway, since a distant aunt had to "take care' of it. He was in Paris, working on the advertisements for a movie his mother was directing, when he got the call.

"Alex, right? It's Cara."

"Layla's Cara?"

Cara's heart skipped a beat.

"Layla's Cara."

None of them said anything for a long minute. Alex felt a sudden, terrible headache.

"I hope I'm not… whee are you right now?" asked Cara.

Alex didn't answer.

"…We won't ever see her again. Someone found my number in her notebook. She… two nights ago… in London… do you understand?"

"I understand," said Alex.

Cara took a deep breath and, with a broken voice, said, *"…the person who called me is the person that Layla spent her last days with. His name is Oscar, and he needs to meet one of us, there in London. Alex, I know I barely ever saw you, but could you do it? I really can't. Scusa."*
Before Alex could say anything, she said, *"You know, a part of me always felt that she was going to end her own life sooner or later, but I never stopped hoping that she would heal."* Cara pronounced these words in a rush, almost as if she didn't want to hear her own words.

"I will do it. I will meet Oscar. Send me the details," he said, before hanging up the phone. Alex

agreed to meet Oscar way earlier than his mind could process the reason behind their meeting. He didn't cry a single tear.
After the call, he kept working nonstop for about seventy hours, when Cara finally sent him Oscar's phone number, then Alex drank all the wine he had left in his living room and headed to the airport.

They met in a cafe.

"*So, how did you know her?*" Alex asked while warming his hands with a hot coffee.
Oscar was a red-haired man in his 20s who studied at Oxford, used dating apps on a daily basis, and had a great sense of fashion. He was deeply obsessed with Frank Sinatra. Most of his talk was about his campus and the Western education he was receiving. He always knew he would end up teaching history at Oxford University someday. He always liked the academic environment, and he often fantasized about having sex on his desk, with whom it didn't matter. Layla blamed his accent and his clothes for wasting her time with him. Perhaps it was his hair or the way he read Shakespeare to her. Perhaps, she wasn't meant to spend her

last days with anyone in particular. Perhaps, she was just a fool, in desperate need of a distraction.

"*I met her in a wine bar near Carnaby Street. It was weird; she wasn't inside the bar. No, she was standing outside the bar with a huge flyer about some local jazz festival, a notebook, and a rose in her hands. I was intrigued by that combination, I think. I asked her if she was interested in drinking wine with an Englishman who could recite her various Shakespeare sonnets by heart.*"

Alex rolled his eyes.

"*... She said she didn't like the idea of Shakespeare coming out of the mouth of a random stranger that much. I said that the wine was on me. She asked me incredibly precise questions in unexpected moments. The first question she asked me was about how I would feel if I happened to be walking on the streets by myself, and then suddenly ran into the bike I used to ride when I was just a little boy... I don't think I ever had a bike...*"

Alex smiled. He kept recognizing his friend in that foreign man's words. Oscar took a sip of tea.

"*...We drank two bottles of red wine that night and then she came to my place, and we spent some days together driving around London and Oxford. We never had sex.*" Oscar took a sip and kept talking,

"...she told me some crazy stories then. At first, I thought she was a liar."

"What did she tell you?" Alex asked.

"She did not tell me her name was Layla right when I met her; in fact, she never told me her name. I saw it on her credit card when she bought her last book. I don't think Layla even noticed the lack of a mention of our names. She also told me that she was feeling bluer than Chet Baker the night we met, then she made a joke about heading to Waterloo Bridge with the intention of jumping, then getting a vegan burrito, and leaving instead... Something of the sort."

Alex stared at Oscar, unaware of what he could ask next and why.

"Who was she?" asked Oscar, interrupting Alex's thoughts. Oscar's questions were fast and sharp, just like his own. He finally understood what Layla meant. They cut straight to the point, like a knife.

Alex thought there was no harm in telling Layla's story now.

"Layla grew up with her father, even though they didn't like or understand each other very much," said Alex in a decreasing voice tone.

"... She rarely talked about her childhood, but I know that the woman who gave birth to her had some problems of some sort. Layla was so disgusted

by her, that in the rare occasions in which she would mention her, she would refer to her as "not Richard, the other one"; I believe it wasn't just a way of neglecting any kind of relationship between her and "the other one", but also a way to underline that, even though she wasn't the biggest fan of Richard, he was still different." Oscar wasn't sure where Alex was getting at with that comment. He was stoned.

"... Growing up, Layla began to fly the country whenever she could, and by the time she turned nineteen, she had already visited half of the European continent. She couldn't stand Italy, and she was always bragging about how the country did dirty to her. I think I might know the reason why, but our lives were so close and so different that it was impossible for me to fully understand, or so she says... she used to say, sorry.

I tried to help her as much as I could. As much as I wanted to. I think it was impossible to help her because no one I know ever loved as much as she did. She loved so much, that lady... she had a box under her bed in which she kept all the letters she wrote but never sent. Each time she left a country she visited, she would leave a letter to a local loved one. Layla loved books, as you might have noticed. I often think of a story she told me once, one of her typical ones. On a sunny day, last year, she was reading Sputnik Sweetheart by Haruki Murakami, sitting on a bus. She then drastically realized she forgot her page markers in her studio; she therefore desired to build her own. She would have held a book she loved and devoured already; cut what she referred to as "some of the best words she ever devoured", then gently glued them to a piece of carton and put the result in the middle of the beloved page. She then, not so drastically, thought she wouldn't cut a book she loved, so she considered making some page markers out of a book she didn't love. What would have been the point then? She couldn't cut something she didn't love," said Alex, thinking about Layla's constant yearning for an overwhelming amount of words. Oscar looked outside the window, completely silent for about two minutes, then eventually opened his mouth.

"*I'm sorry,*" he said, still stoned.

He wanted to tell Alex that, when he first met Layla, he was under the impression of three things. Number One. She loved Chet Baker. For some reason, Oscar was convinced she was listening to *"My Funny Valentine"* with her headphones on when he met her. He never asked, so that she could never deny it. The fact that Layla then mentioned *"born to be blue"* did nothing but fuel his delusions.

Number Two. She had quite an unconventional relationship with her mother country, which was now proven to be true.

Number Three. Oscar knew, no matter how hard he would try, that Layla was looking for a feeling that he did not have in him.

Alex rushed out of the bar. "*What a useless thing to be sorry,*" he thought. "*I'm sorry,*" Alex said out loud. He entered a bakery, had a cake, took a knife in his hand, and smashed the cake till there was no more. The waitress was terrified. Maybe he told Oscar too much about her. Then again, Oscar had to know, since he spent her last days with her. Oscar was there, and no one else. That was unfair. That was betrayal.

One particular thing Alex said was true. Layla loved a lot. She felt so much love, she had no idea where to place it. It was heavy and bloody, and it was all hers. It was not the kind of property that could satisfy her in any way, hence she yearned to get rid of it. She wanted to get rid of it in the morning, when, as soon as she woke up, *Love* was already weighing heavily on her. She wanted to get rid of it at breakfast, regardless of her willingness to cook. She could cook differently, for *Love*. She wanted to get rid of it when she was with her friends, who loved each other enough to share an apartment and dedicate themselves to each other every day of their lives. She wanted to get rid of this *Love* while waiting for the bus, and while traveling on a train, whether it was on time, late, or stuck in the same station for far too long. She knew somewhere, some lover was waiting for someone who was on that train. She wanted to get rid of this *Love* during concerts, when people held hands as they screamed together, and afterwards, on her way back home, wet by the rain and by her solitude. She wanted to get rid of it while kissing: it could then turn deadly. It made it impossible for her to live; this *Love* she needed to get rid of.

"How does one do that? The others, all of this Love, where do they keep it?"

Chapter XI.
Such a boring lad (Mood Indigo)

The sun rose and set twice on Bond Street, as Alex felt stuck in London. He just extended his booking for one whole week; he wasn't sure why.

Finally, something to reason his stay came up: Oscar called Alex and decided to give him the black bag Layla left at his place. He forgot to bring it when they met at the cafe, slightly overwhelmed by the task. Her diary must have been inside it. Oscar's apartment was reachable by train. Alex decided to take the train when the sun began to set, so that he could witness the lights inside the apartments he was passing by. Most of them seemed welcoming, even from the train's window, just as Alex liked. One thing he couldn't stand was the so-called "*office lights*"; they made him think of hospitals and corporations. It doesn't really get worse than that. He truly enjoyed spying on these people's lives from afar, judging their light-related choices and imagining the music that would be

playing in their apartments, as well as the smells that filled their kitchens.
How many of those apartments were a home? Which ones were just buildings, and how does one make up that difference?

Alex almost forgot to get off the train, immersed in his thoughts. But he didn't. He walked out, *minded the gap*, and headed towards a stranger's apartment. A stranger whom someone he loved spent her last days with. Alex wouldn't admit it to himself, but he was mad at Layla for giving up. He couldn't understand it. It didn't make sense.

He knew Layla loved life, for that time that Layla asked him to go for a swim during *the last sunset in Autumn*, just two or three years prior to that cold London night.

"No way. I have an important screening in a week. It is cold, and I am not getting sick."

"But, Alex, it's the last sunset of this Autumn!", exclaimed Layla.

"That's not even a thing," Alex replied.

"It's a thing if you make it a thing. Please, Alex! Don't make me go alone. Compared to you, who will probably start shouting once his feet touch the water, I will look like a strong lady who fears nothing. Plus, we don't even have class tomorrow."

"Layla, you are a strong Lady who fears nothing. So go alone," he had concluded.

That memory felt way more distant now than the week before, when Alex didn't know Layla was not Layla anymore. One moment your memory is alive - and so are you, and the next it's not - and so you aren't. Perhaps, the real death is not about the memory related to the dead, but the memories that the dead had in mind and that won't be played again.

Oscar's apartment was on the third floor. As you entered it, you wouldn't notice anything in particular. Alex wondered why Layla, out of all the people in London, found Oscar. Such a boring lad. The walls were white, the chairs were made of wood and painted white, and so was the table. The apartment had a parquet floor that seemed untouched, given how clean it was. Oscar opened the door with only a pair of trousers on. He wasn't even wearing his eyeglasses. It was unusual to spot Oscar without glasses - they were the only thing lying on the white table that Alex could spot from the door.

"I am sorry, I am gonna have a long day tomorrow, would you mind taking her bag with you and going?" said Oscar.

He wouldn't even mention her name. How dare he? To him, Layla was a stranger, and he wouldn't mention her name. A stranger she died with.

Oscar handed Alex Layla's bag before Alex could even nod. He opened the diary and threw the bag on the floor. He couldn't wait to get his final answers. The last bloody question he would ever ask her: *why?*

"I don't want to be here anymore. I cannot control them. I cannot control them. I cannot. I can't control my hands. My own hands are trying to murder me: I tried wearing gloves, surrounding them with plastic, getting them busy - yet they are still thirsty for my own blood.

Someone is yelling something about a fish and chips and table five, and my hands are still thirsty for my blood. I can't believe all of those people are real: my colleagues, the guests, everyone else. I am interacting with them, and they still don't know anything, as I don't know anything about them. I don't know anything about anyone.

I cannot control my hands..."

"... I spent the entire day crawling on the floor. I am crazy. I feel... distant from this floor, distant from this planet. Is that why I am crawling on the ground? to feel closer to the Earth that birthed me? For all my life, I tried to be a human, I tried to be a person, I tried to connect with other humans, but right now I wouldn't even know how to express my truest self to them. I am not sure I am a part of anything except my art, which I cannot even define, and which AI might take over soon. I am just a lost entity occupying space, fulfilling my days by vomiting drawings.
When I was younger, I had a sticker pack that I never attached anywhere because I was too scared to ruin it. I blame Richard for that; Once, he spotted me trying to put a new sticker on my wardrobe, and he stopped me and said that I should save it. Save it for what? What would I do with a sticker of a little bear, now? Things get ruined whether you consume them or not: stickers, clothes, ideas, people... I intend to consume myself. I will have a good life. I need to. I will truly live a consuming life. I will do my best to burn. Then again, Hedonism will always fail as long as dreams won't last as much as reality does."

"Soon, I will grow old. I am giving myself quite a life. I do my best, I do. I pay the price of not having a home. Soon, I will grow old. It doesn't mean much, except, I am now a person. I am now a woman.
I am longing for Paris. I wanna dance in New Orleans. I wanna run in Berlin. I want to surf in Agadir. I want to walk around Torino. I want to

draw strangers in Damascus. I want to fall in love in Vienna. I want to eat in Oaxaca. I want to fall asleep in Napoli, cradled by the joyful voices of my neighbours. I want to drink chai in Tehran. I want to read by the water in Stockholm. I want to cry here. I want to go home."

Alex was still standing in front of Oscar's door when he read those words. He could easily picture Layla writing all of that. He wasn't mad anymore.

"Alex, I have a question for you. I mean, not for you as yourself, but for you as the only person I can ask this to…"

Alex shut the door and left fast, before Oscar could finish his sentence. There was nothing that Oscar could say that could bring Layla back. He then headed to a bench near the Thames and read every page of Layla's diary before throwing it into the water.

www.ingramcontent.com/pod-product-compliance
Lightning Source LLC
La Vergne TN
LVHW020511100826
845148LV00003B/753

* 9 7 8 9 4 0 3 8 6 1 8 4 5 *